He Loves Me,

He Loves You Not

A Novel By

Mychea

GOOD2GO PUBLISHING

Published by:
GOOD2GO PUBLISHING
7311 W. Glass Lane
Laveen, AZ 85339
www.good2gopublishing.com
twitter @good2gobooks
G2G@good2gopublishing.com
Facebook.com/good2gopublishing
ThirdLane Marketing: Brian James
Brian@good2gopublishing.com

Cover design: Davida Baldwin
Typesetter: Rukyyah
ISBN: 978-0-615-52597-6

ACKNOWLEDGEMENTS

Special thanks to Silk White for his belief in my talent.
Many, many thanks to my family and friends for their continual support.
Lots of hugs and kisses to my loyal fans. You guys rock!!
~M~

Prologue

"I fucking love you so much that I hate your ass now."

He said as a sole tear dripped down his face, "It wasn't just sex with me and you. It was love making no matter how cheap you tried to make me feel." His words were laced with heartfelt emotion as he pulled the telephone cord tighter around her neck and watched her breathe her last breath. Staring into her eyes as her life slipped away was an intimate bounding experience for him. He felt closer to her now than he did the numerous times they had made love.

Uncoiling the cord, he gazed down in satisfaction admiring his work. Her lifeless face stared back at him. She'd never looked more beautiful than she did right now with her blue and black bruised body lying on the floor. Giving her a proper farewell, he picked her up off the floor and kissed her lifeless lips, wishing she had made the right decision that could have led to hot sex with each other on an isolated island somewhere.

Placing her motionless body next to her husband's, he was finally glad to be done with her and her lies. How dare she think she could tell him the truth after all this time and walk away from their arrangement as if it never happened? As if what they'd shared hadn't been real or good enough in her eyes? He wanted to dedicate his life to her and make it work. Living in her world more than he lived in his own with his wife, she still hadn't felt that he'd been worthy of all of her, where they could leave their inconvenient marriages behind and be as one together. She'd been selfishly trying to have it all, him and her own family. He'd never thought in a million years that she wouldn't choose a life with him. He'd thought what they shared was more special than what their spouses were giving them.

Gazing down at her husband's lifeless body, he felt like he had done them both justice. Now, her husband no longer had to be enslaved with her lies either. He set them all free. Smiling as he grabbed the gas can and drenched the room with gasoline; he was extremely pleased with himself. Lighting a cigarette, he relished in the calmness of the night, immune to the dead bodies lying around him. There would never be another woman whom he would allow to get to him like this one did. Never. Taking one last puff off his cigarette, he began his retreat towards the door, stopping only to light a match and flick it behind him in the darkened room. As he made his exit into the eerily still night, not even the moon illuminated the dreary sky. All that could be seen, in the distance, was the solitary house going ablaze.

Chapter One

Feeling the scraping of her scalp as the last bobby pin was placed in Shia's up do; she grimaced a little but didn't utter a word. Her sense of urgency was too great. She was marrying the man of her dreams and nothing compared to that. The only thing that could make today better was if her parents could be here to see.

"Come on Shy, you need to get your makeup done and into your dress." Remi said as she walked out into the garden at the Overhill's mansion in Baltimore, Maryland where Shia was standing taking in the calm serenity of her wedding site.

"Ok, ok." Shia smiled as Remi rushed her out of the garden and whisked her into the dressing room where the make-up artist was waiting.

Unlike the calmness Shia was feeling, Leigh on the other hand was running around frantic. Guests were arriving at the church, bridesmaids were losing bouquets, and the groom and groomsmen were nowhere to be found. Leigh would be lying if she said she wasn't in full-blown panic mode. Looking down as Shia's cell began to vibrate in her hand; she breathed a sigh of relief when Shia's fiancé Trent's name flashed across the screen.

"Where the hell are you?" Leigh screeched into the phone when she answered.

"Lemme speak to Shy." Trent responded ignoring her question.

"She's getting her makeup done and about to get dressed. I'll see you in a few." Leigh said hanging up the phone. Shia didn't have time for Trent's "I love you's." Leigh felt that she needed to focus on getting ready to walk down the aisle.

Stepping back in the dressing room, Leigh stopped short.

"Oh my God Shy," Leigh exclaimed with tears in her eyes, "You look beautiful." And she truly was. Her hair was swept up in a pin up with soft curls framing her face. Her veil cascaded down her back. Shia was decked out in a Silk Shantung, pleated A-line gown from the Casablanca Bridal Couture line. Her makeup was flawless. She looked like a model.

"You look just like Mom used to look when we were younger." Leigh said handing Shia her bouquet.

"Thanks. I'm so nervous and anxious at the same time." She turned to look at herself in the mirror. "I can't wait to marry Trent. This is the happiest day of my life."

"I know it is and I am so happy for you! You already know I think Trent is an amazing guy." Leigh replied giving Shia a hug.

"Awww, I'm missing the sister moment." Remi said entering the dressing room, "Let me in you guys." Leigh and Shia laughed as they extended their hug to include her.

"Ok chicks, get off me." Leigh laughed stepping out of their embrace. They knew she wasn't the hugging, affectionate type.

"Shy, the ushers need to know where the programs are. You should have told me I had to do all this legwork. Got me running back and forth looking crazy." Remi laughed.

"Hush, you do not look crazy." Shia smiled at her, "The programs should be in the trunk of my car. My keys are in my purse by the door. Can you get them and give them to the ushers please?"

"Your wish is my command. Guess I'm your genie for the day." Remi snickered as she grabbed the keys out of Shia's purse and left the room.

Shia shook her head and laughed before turning her attention to Leigh.

"Lei Lei, is Trent here yet?"

"Oh, yeah, no he's not here, but he called, and I told him to get dressed and we'll see him when he gets here."

"Leigh, give me my phone," Shia said in slight annoyance as Leigh handed her the phone and she dialed Trent's number and held the phone to her ear, "You should have given it to me when he called. I always wanna talk to my man."

Hearing the phone stop ringing as if picked up, Shia spoke first.

"Hi baby. I love you."

"Yeah, no baby here." Hearing the woman's familiar voice on the other end of the line, Shia could feel her annoyance turning into anger as she quickly glanced down at the phone confirming that she had dialed the right number.

"Umm, excuse me." Shia said into the phone, unwilling to believe that she had heard the voice she thought she did.

"Shia, this is Phylicia. You know you recognize my voice so cut the games. Trent's busy running our bath water."

"What?" Shia said in a voice of disbelief with an attitude. She was angry and irritated. Why in the world did Phylicia have Trent's phone. She couldn't help thinking the worse. "Phylicia, stop playing."

"No games involved. You heard me right the first time. He's running our bath water. I know you think you're getting married today, unfortunately that isn't going to happen. Sorry." Phylicia said hanging up the phone in her ear.

"Shy, what's wrong?"

Tears raced down Shia's face as she felt like there wasn't enough air supply in the room. Letting the phone drop to the floor and attempting to suck in air, she found it hard to speak.

"He, he's not coming." She managed to whisper in between breaths.

"He's what?" Leigh's eyes grew the size of saucers, "What the hell do you mean?"

"With Phylicia," she gasped out.

Leigh's eyes grew big, "That dumb bitch!" she screamed. Shia couldn't breathe. "Oh my God. Get me out of this dress. Please, please." Shia begged, "I can't breathe." She began frantically clawing at the dress trying to get it off.

Leigh was so mad she was seeing different shades of red and sad for Shia all at once.

"I could kill Trent. How dare he do this to you?"

“Ok Shy, I’m a help you out the dress as fast as I can.” Leigh grabbed the scissors from the hairdresser’s stand, angrily cut Shia out of her gown, and watched nine thousand dollars of couture hit the ground. Shia promptly slid to the floor.

“What’s wrong with her?” Remi asked Leigh as she walked back into the room and saw Shia sitting in the middle of the floor crying. “Why did you cut her dress?”

Leigh and Remi watched as Shia jumped up and ran into the bathroom shutting the door firmly behind her.

“Trent’s not coming. There isn’t going to be a wedding.”

“Huh?” Remi said with a dumb face, “Come again.”

“No wedding!” Leigh said louder this time, “One of us needs to go out there and tell all the guests.”

"I mean what is happening? I stepped out of the room for two seconds." Remi asked Leigh as she shook her head in disbelief, "I can make the announcement, but what should I say to all those people?"

"Shia will have to explain everything later. Right now, you'll have to make up something." Leigh answered her. She walked over to the bathroom door as she watched a confused Remi leave the room.

Knocking on the door, Leigh waited for Shia to respond, but got no reply.

Shia heard the knock at the door but couldn’t bring herself to answer. Sitting on the floor by the sink, she buried her head into her hands. She was in shock, not believing that Trent would do this to her on their wedding day. He didn’t even have the decency to show up and tell her himself. After everything that they had gone through together, her heart was breaking into a million pieces and she knew there would be no fixing it this time.

THE PAST

Chapter Two

Winter 2004

Setting the last of the moving boxes on the living room floor, Trent rotated his shoulders back slowly. He was happy to be done. Retrieving a beer from the fridge, he flopped down on the couch, cutting ESPN on his 70' LED T.V. He was glad he'd had Time Warner set up the cable on the same day he was moving in. Catching Sports Center, he was happy to see the highlights from the Cowboys and Giants game that he'd missed. Throwing his hands into the air, Trent cheered when he saw the resulting score. The Giants shut them Boys down once again. Tossing his beer into the trash can as he got up to answer the ringing phone; he was in the best mood.

"Speak." He said into his cell.

"What's up T? What you up to?" Trent smiled when he heard his boy Kodi's voice on the other end.

"What you mean?" Trent asked as he flopped back down on the couch, "I've been moving all day, remember. You were supposed to be here helping me?"

"My bad. Yo, Sherri hit me up and I had to make a quick stop at home really fast."

Trent looked down at his watch, "Man. It's ten after five; you were supposed to meet me at eight this morning."

"I thought it was gonna be quick, but Sherri had some new tricks for your boy. You know I couldn't leave until I got all that."

Trent shook his head, "You too old to still be chasing cat. You need to leave Sherri's crazy ass alone."

"Oh, I forgot. Your playa card was taken from you. My bad, but don't hate on your boy. I'm just one squirrel in this great big forest of women, trying to bust a nut."

"You keep playing with crazy ass Sherri and your nuts gonna be cut off."

"Yeah man, I hear you. Check this," Kodi said moving on in the conversation, "What you doing tonight? Let's hit up Haze. You know its Valentine's Day weekend, so all the single bitches gonna be there looking for something to get into or someone to get in them."

Trent shook his head again, "And you want to be that someone, don't you?"

"Hey, I can't bless them all, but I can let a few get a piece of the god."

"I don't know. I have a lot of boxes to unpack an—"

"Man, kill that noise. Them boxes ain't going nowhere. When was the last time you hung with your boy? You a free man now. We need to celebrate."

Thinking it over for a moment, Trent realized that it was a while since he'd hung out with his man Kodi. Unpacking boxes could wait. Kodi was right. They weren't going anywhere.

"Aight, I'll go. Give me some time to hop into the shower and shave, and I'll meet you down there around eleven."

"Bet. See you then."

Trent made it to Club Haze a little after eleven and as usual, Kodi was running late. He'd just sent him a text saying he'd been tied up but was on his way. All Trent could do was shake his head. He knew that meant Kodi was off getting some from one of his women. He wondered when his friend would learn.

Trent stopped chasing the cat in his early-twenties. Last year at the age of twenty-five when he'd met Phylicia, she had shown him how good it could be when a woman loved you and he could appreciate it. She'd been special. So special that he'd proposed to her. Everything was perfect until she became pregnant. That's when all hell broke loose. At first, he'd been excited to find out about the baby, but things slowly started to happen. He learned Phylicia was married and once the baby was born, they'd had her paternity tested and learned the baby girl was Phylicia's husband seed. Women could be so devious. The hurting part was Phylicia and he was living together. That jacked up situation prompted his move to the Upper West Side of Manhattan on West 71st Street. A fresh start was what he needed and what he intended to get.

Jumping when he heard tapping on his car window, Trent turned swiftly and saw Kodi standing there cheesing. Turning his car off, Trent got out.

"Man, don't be banging on my window at night. Mess around and get shot."

"Your Mr. Clean ass ain't gonna do shit." Kodi said laughing, "Let's go up in this spot so these women can be in the presence of a god."

Trent chuckled to himself. Some people would never change. Kodi was one of them. Ever since they were kids playing in daycare together, Trent remembered how Kodi used to hit all the girls he liked making them cry. It seemed like his knowledge of women didn't improve with age.

When they entered, the club was jumping as usual. Trent hadn't been in years and he could see that he hadn't missed anything. He noticed the same type of women were still there. The glammed up women who had spent their last dime on their new outfit, who would be looking for guys to buy them drinks all night. Then there were the women who strictly came to get their freak on. The ones that rubbed up on your dick all night, then when you try to take them home afterwards, they screamed they had a man and making a guy want to say, "Your ass wasn't acting like you had one in there, but aight, keep it moving." Then you had the I'm a fuck you right here, right now woman. Trent always tried to stay away from those women, whenever they were willing to give it up that easily, he was just as dead set on keeping it in his pants even more. Lastly, you had the woman who was dragged there by her friends. You could see it in her face. She wore a sign on her forehead that said, "Fuck Off." She didn't socialize with anyone, walked around with an attitude, and generally held up a bar spot or just stood against the wall taking up space. Trent shook his head in disgust. It was still the same scene, just a different day.

"Yo, look at all the sexy women in this place." Kodi said as Trent glanced around. Some of the women were ok, but none of them had anything on Phylicia's lying, cheating ass. She was gorgeous and her game was tight. That's how she'd been able to reel him in.

He remembered the first time he'd seen Phylicia. He was at the Brooklyn museum with another woman who was irking the shit out of him that day and he'd been looking for a way to ditch her. When she'd said she wanted to gaze at a particular piece she liked a bit longer, Trent had gladly walked away to relieve himself of her presence, as well as look at other art.
Rounding the corner, Trent stopped short; there she was. She must have dropped her purse because it lip-gloss, pens, make-up and paper were everywhere. Retrieving her cell, which was next to his foot, Trent approached the amazing looking woman.

"I believe this is yours." He said squatting down next to her.
Glancing up at him, she blushed. Reaching her hand out to grab the phone, she said, "I apologize for it being in the way." She paused as she took all of him in, "I can be such a klutz sometimes."
Gazing into her chocolate almond-shaped eyes, Trent stuck out his hand, "Hi, I'm Trent."

Taking his hand into hers slowly, she said, "Hello, I'm Phylicia," she smiled, "And thanks again for retrieving my phone."

"Not a problem," he replied as he helped her pick up the rest of her things. Lazily standing back to his feet, he reached for her hand to help her rise when they were done.

"I can't thank you enough. What can I do to show my appreciation for your generosity?"

One side of Trent's mouth turned up in a half grin. She had afforded him the perfect opening. Gazing down into her beautiful face, he took in all of her features. She was tall with an athletic build and a round ass. She reminded him of the actress Salli Richardson.

"You can have dinner with me tonight." He responded.

"Oh, I don't know about that." She said averting her eyes. Trent shrugged pulling out his business card, "Call me if you change your mind." He said handing her his card then walking away to find his date.

"Hello?" Trent cautiously answered his cell phone on the second ring. He was apprehensive about answering numbers he didn't know.

"Hi." A soft milk chocolate voice responded, "This is Phylicia. We met at the Brooklyn Museum."

Phylicia, Trent thought. How could he forget about the woman he met about two weeks ago?

"Phylicia, nice to hear from you. I guess you changed your mind, huh?"

There was a small pause on her end, "I guess so."

"What can I do for you?"

"Well, I was phoning to see if you would be available later this evening."

Trent quickly checked his calendar. He was supposed to go out with Kodi to a new lounge opening in Manhattan, but he was sure Kodi would understand if he cancelled, as much as that dude liked to chase the cat.

"I'm available."

"Wonderful! Text me your address and I'll pick you up around seven."

Trent was shocked that she wanted to pick him up. He couldn't recall a woman ever offering to do that before. He hadn't even had dinner with her yet and her stock value had already increased as far as he was concerned.

"Sounds like a bet. See you at seven."

"Aye, come with me real quick, I left my phone and shit in the car." Kodi said as he interrupted Trent's thoughts once again.

Trent sighed as he bounced back to reality letting the memory of Phylicia fade as he followed Kodi out the club.

Chapter Three

The bus gave a sudden jolt as it began inching its way through traffic again. Shia groaned aloud. She loved her twin sister Leigh, but traveling from DC to New York by bus and being stuck in the Lincoln tunnel every time was starting to wear on her nerves.

It was Valentine's Day weekend and Leigh wanted Shia to come spend it with her since she didn't have anyone special to spend Valentine's Day with. Shia realized how pathetic that seemed, but who could be a better date than her sister, she thought. It was better than staying home alone with no one to cuddle up to she convinced herself as she cruised along on the Mega Bus in the dead of winter headed to New York City to party or better yet, to forget the fact that she was single for yet another Valentine's Day. Sighing as she looked out the window at the bright lights of the New York City skyline, Shia couldn't wait to say good-bye to this god-awful bus so her weekend adventure could begin.

Having arrived at Leigh's apartment a little after eight in the evening; just in time to get ready for their club night, Shia was dressed and ready to go. Peeping herself in the mirror, she knew she looked good. Her mother used to say that she and Leigh were carbon copies of the Sister Sister television stars twins Tia and Tamara Mowry. At twenty-four years of age, standing at an even 5'4 Shia was in perfect shape. Her five a.m. four mile runs every day had given her body the extra toning it needed to look statuesque in her curve hugging black dress.

"Leigh, what is taking you so long?" Shia yelled to Leigh, who was in the bathroom.

Finally, opening up the door, Leigh rushed out in her towel.

"You have got to be kidding me. You've been in there all that time and you're still in your towel? I didn't come all this way to sit in your apartment and watch you parade around with no clothes on."

"Shia, I know. Ease up on me, ok. You know my hair takes a minute and then my whole make-up ritual."

"That's the problem right there. You wear too much make-up and you don't need it." Shia was telling the truth, Leigh really didn't need a lot of make-up she was pretty enough without it.

"You should go natural like me. Some lip gloss and I'm done."

"Well excuse me, we don't all have that luxury. I know we're twins and all, but a sister needs a perm. I didn't get naturally silky hair like you did."

Shia laughed at Leigh. "Hey, you have my face. I'm entitled to something aren't I?"

Leigh smiled and rolled her eyes, "Girl, you so crazy. What are you wearing tonight?"

Holding up an ultra short bright red strapless dress that had see through lace stripes going through it both of Shia's eyebrows shot up.

"This! What do you think?"

"Oh my God! All your goodies gonna be hanging out. That is not a dress, that is a piece of cloth."

"Stop being such a prude. Yours is only a little longer than mine."

"Yeah, but it doesn't have all those pieces cut out like yours does."

Sliding into the dress, Leigh gave Shia the whatever look. She was going to rock the hell out of her dress tonight.

Glancing down at the time on her cell phone Leigh huffed for about the fifth time. I can't believe we are still standing in this line."

"Now you knew when we set out this evening that we would have to stand in line." Shia told her, though she secretly agreed. They was in line for well over an hour. This was one of the reasons why she usually didn't go to the club. The only good thing was the line kept inching forward slowly, so they were making a steady progress, be it a slow one.

Shia watched as two very handsome men walked past them straight to the door. Before she could think twice, she jumped out of line, grabbing Leigh as she walked up behind the two men.

"What in the world are you doing?" Leigh hissed, "Now we've lost our place in line."

Ignoring her, Shia tapped the taller gentleman on the shoulder.

"Hi, I'm Shia." She said sticking out her hand.

Trent turned when he felt the tap on his back and looked down at the pretty woman extending her hand for him to shake.

Mesmerized by her full pouty lips, Trent reached out his hand to meet hers, but couldn't remember what she said her name was.

"I'm sorry. I missed your name."

"It's Shia." She repeated gracefully. "And this is my sister Leigh." She said pointing at the identical woman with lots of hair and make-up, body screaming sex me. The type of woman Kodi liked.

Trent wasn't bothered by their presence. He just wondered where they came from. Glancing back at the rather long line to get into the club, he put two & two together. Releasing Shia's hand, he gazed into her eyes, offering up a slight smile.

"Tired of standing in line by chance?"

Blushing slightly because she had so easily been found out, "Uh, see, umm," Shia stumbled over her words.

Trent chuckled softly. "It's ok; you and your sister can come in with us. I'm sure my man won't mind."

Turning back to Kodi, who was engaged in conversation with the club owner, Trent interrupted.

"Hey K, is it cool if these ladies join us?"

Peeping around Trent, Kodi wanted to see what the ladies were working with. Smiling, he nodded his approval. He could tell that the night was definitely going to be a good one.

"Shy, I can't believe you got us out that long ass line." Leigh yelled over the music.

"It's called taking the initiative and hoping they don't turn us away." Shia laughed. The two men had them into the club with them and were now getting drinks from the bar.

"Turn us away? Please." Leigh eyed Shia incredulously, "Did you see the way Trent looked at you? Brotha man was a goner on your arrival. Don't think I didn't see him slid you his phone number."

Shia felt the color rise on her cheeks. She embarrassed easy, "Leigh, hush your mouth. He was no such thing and so what if he did give me his number?"

"Stop being so uptight all your life." Shia instantly took offense. She hated when Leigh called her uptight.

Shia gave her the evil eye, "Yeah, well I see how you and Kodi keep sniggling and giggling over there. For once, try to keep it tight. Guys like him are only after one thing. Don't get caught up in it."

"Dag I thought I left my mother at home. I got this, aight. You just worry about yourself."

"Whatever," Shia mumbled dropping the subject since the men were rejoining them with drinks.

Shia shook her head in disgust when Leigh hopped onto Kodi's lap as he held the cup for her to drink from his hands.

"They seem to be hitting it off well," Trent said nodding in the two's direction.

Shia shrugged, "Yeah. I guess." She wasn't interested in what Leigh was doing at this point. Though she did want to know more about Trent.

"Tell me something about you." She said softly to him.

"What do you want to know?"

"What do you want to tell me?" She asked playfully.

"I'm not really good at playing games. If you want to know something, then ask."

Shia was taken back a little. "Ok," she began slowly, "Why are you here, at the club? You don't seem like the clubbing type, unlike your boy over there, "She pointed over at Kodi as Leigh was giving him a lap dance."Who seems like he enjoys this type of thing?"

“Kodi suggested we come out to celebrate and just hang. It’s been a while since we hung out. But to be honest, you're right. I'm not the clubbing type.”

“Yeah, it’s not really my scene either. But Leigh loves this type of thing,” Shia said nodding disapprovingly toward her sister as she watched Kodi’s hand creeping its way up Leigh’s short dress.

“Excuse me, but it’s nice to see you out and smiling again.”

Shia glanced up at the sound of the voice to see who was interrupting them. “Hey Phylicia,” Trent said standing up, “What are you doing here?”

Phylicia narrowed her eyes at the woman who was sitting next to Trent in their cozy little VIP section. Shia ignored the woman and continued sipping her drink.

“You’re dating another woman already; at least I think that’s what you would call her.”

Leigh jumped up off Kodi’s lap when she heard that, “Aye bitch you better cool off. You don’t know us like that.”

“Leigh, leave it alone,” Shia said taking another sip from her drink, “She’s not worth the argument.”

“What the fuck you say?” Phylicia yelled trying to step around Trent to get at the woman.

Grabbing Phylicia by the arm, Trent pulled her alongside him and walked out of the VIP section.

“What the hell is wrong with you?” He finally said once he got her in a corner pressed up against the wall, “Why you in here trying to cause problems?”

“Why are you in here with another woman? What are you trying to prove?”

Trent laughed at Phylicia in spite of himself, because the drama she was pulling wasn't in the least bit funny.

"I don't have to prove anything, especially to you. Just stay out of my way and don't come in here with your mess. I'm just trying to have a good time. Shouldn't you be home with your husband and baby?"

"I'm legally separated now."

"Send my congrats to your husband."

Phylicia felt tears welling up in her eyes, "Baby, why are you being so mean?"

"Kill the drama and the tears; they don't work on me anymore." Trent shook his head in disbelief. Phylicia was definitely still beautiful, there was no denying that, but she was poison. He had survived her vicious bite the first time; he wasn't so sure he would survive a second.

"So who is that woman you're with? I know you can't have found someone so soon."

"Soon? It's been three months. Don't worry about who she is and I've been rude long enough. Stay away from me. You're like kryptonite. You kill everything around you."

"Trent, if you walk away from me, we are done forever."

"Is that a promise?" Trent replied as he left Phylicia standing on the wall with her mouth hanging open in disbelief. Returning to he and Kodi's section, he was surprised to see the twins were gone and Kodi was sitting with another woman on his lap.

Kodi saw Trent and his face broke into a smile. "They left, so I moved on. Got one for you too." Kodi said nodding in the direction of another petite woman answering Trent's question before he had a chance to ask where the women went.

Chapter Four

Trent had everything going great in his life. Working for NYC Marketing, Inc proved to be very lucrative for him. All he was missing was a woman in his life. He didn't lack for women. At this stage in the game, all he needed was one good woman and he thought he had that. But he needed a woman whom he could count on if shit hit the fan, like him losing his job or if anything unexpected happened, not a woman who didn't have the first idea of what being in a relationship was all about. Phylicia was the perfect woman. She had really messed his mind up.

"I need a vacation. My job has been kicking my ass lately. I always have to hand walk my clients through why they need marketing services and how beneficial it is to have a business plan in effect. It's draining. I just want to relax once in a while, you feel me?" Trent told Kodi. The two had met up at Blondies Sports Bar on West 79th Street for a quick after work drink.

"Nah, you just need some bomb ass head. Man, I got this shorty down the way that can wax your shit so good; she'll make you forget you even got a job."

Shaking his head, Trent laughed. That was Kodi being Kodi. Always got that cat on his brain. It didn't matter what they were talking about, somehow the conversation always made its way back to something sexual.

"Man, you crazy. I gets mine. All I'm saying is that I need a break. I'm ready for something else you know."

"Like what, shit you have damn near everything. What else you need?"

"I think I'm ready to settle down."

Kodi looked at Trent as if he had two heads or something. "Why would you want ta do some dumb shit like that? You just got done with Phylicia's trifling ass. You at your prime right now, you could have hoes busting down your door and shit, if you ever took your ass out the crib." Kodi took a swig from his beer, "Man you trippin'."

"After the situation with Phylicia, I need to step my woman game up. Shit is getting out of control. I had this one shortie that was bold enough to research my ass and show up at my Momma house." Trent stared down at his drink, "I'm just tired of this crazy stuff all the time, you know? I need peace."

"Damn, you had a shortie hit up your Moms spot. Yeah, that bitch would have had to go. I hope you cut her ass back."

Trent smirked as he took a sip out of his glass, "Nah."

Kodi gave Trent the crazy look, "Why the hell not?"

"She got that bomb ass head." Trent said and began cracking up. Kodi joined in. Trent couldn't help himself, being with Kodi always brought out that other side of him. He still didn't chase women like his boy, but he was single, so if one were willing to give it up that he was worth his time he would indulge himself from time to time.

"I can understand that shit, but I still would have had to let her ass know. Poppin' up at Moms house is no good. T man, you gotta train your bitches so that shit don't happen."

"Man, they not all bitches, it's just that the ones that are, usually do the best tricks. That's why we put up with their crazy asses."

Shaking his head as if reminiscing, Kodi tossed back the rest of his beer, "Shit, you right."

Feeling his iPhone vibrating at his hip, Trent frowned when he saw Phylicia's name pop up. He hadn't spoken to her since the night she had shown up unexpectedly at Club Haze. He guessed forever hadn't come yet, since she was still contacting him.

Hitting ignore on his phone, he took another sip from his drink, trying to focus on what Kodi was saying. Looking down as his phone began vibrating again, Trent saw Phylicia's name flash across the screen.

"Damn," he mumbled under his breath, "When will she leave me alone?"

"What's wrong with you?"

"Phylicia keeps hitting me up." Trent said disgusted at the situation as he downed the rest of his drink. "You see what I'm saying? I need peace."

"Whatever happened with you and ol' girl?"

Trent knew exactly who Kodi was referring to.

"I haven't spoken to her since the night at Haze after Phylicia's crazy ass showed up and she dipped out. Figured she didn't want to be bothered with my drama."

"You don't know till you try. She seemed cool, unlike her sister, who is psycho and now that the God has blessed her. I can't get rid of the bitch."

Trent shook his head; he couldn't see how Kodi kept up with his women. He had summed up Leigh when he met her and knew she would be trouble. Everything about her screamed come sex me. Those are always the ones to bring drama. That must be how Kodi liked them. Those were the women he continuously pursued.

"What is she doing to you?"

Pausing to ask the bartender for another drink, Kodi answered, "She just be doing dumb shit. When I first went to her house, she was cool, but then shortie starting getting attached and clingy. Calling and texting my phone all hours of the night. You know Sherry not having that shit. I swear this bitch been following me. Nothing I can prove yet, just a hunch."

"You the police, have someone watch her." Trent suggested.

"Nah, I gotta have a reason to do something like that."

"See why I don't need a whole bunch of women busting my door down." Trent pointed out. "I don't need more problems than I have now."

"Whatever man. She might have been worth it if the sex was good, but she can't even give the god a decent head job. She actually bit my shit and thought I would like that shit." Kodi was getting more and more disgusted thinking about it. "There's nothing she can do for me. I want her gone."

"You always get yourself caught up in these crazy situations. Need to stop going all out on these women, give them a piece of the dick, not all of it."

Kodi smirked, "If you get the opportunity to be in the god's presence, you're entitled to all of it."

Laughing, Trent took a sip from the drink the bartender had sat in front of him. "Aight 'God' keep dealing with these crazies then." He raised his arm as if to toast him, "Good luck with that." He said as his phone began to vibrate again. This time he answered.

"Yo."

"Can we talk please?"

"No." He responded to Phylicia's pleading voice.

"Trent, stop acting like this. Please just hear me out."

"What Phylicia? You starting to irritate me."

"All I'm asking is that you come over so we can talk."

Kodi must have known Phylicia was bringing it strong, because when Trent looked up at him, he was waving his hands back and forth frantically mouthing, "Don't do it."

Laughing silently, he turned his back on Kodi, so he could focus on what Phylicia was saying.

"I can cook you dinner." He heard her say.

"As great as that sounds, I'm going to have to decline."

"Trent, all I'm asking for is some of your time. Just for us to clear the air. I don't want to leave things on a sour note."

Sighing, seeing as how she would probably harass him until she got her way. Trent gave in.

"Aight Phylicia. I'll stop by on my way home tonight."

"Thanks. I really appreciate this. You have no idea."

"I bet. Talk to you later." He said hanging up.

When he turned around, Kodi was standing there shaking his head back and forth.

"She got you right where she wants you bruh. Good Luck."

"Thanks," Trent replied setting his empty glass on the bar, "I'm going to need it."

* * * *

Pulling up to Phylicia's Brooklyn apartment, Trent could already sense the tension that was waiting for him upstairs. He didn't even know why he was here to begin with. There was nothing that Phylicia could say to him that would make him take her back. Nothing at all, but for whatever reason, he needed to hear what she had to say. Exiting his truck slowly, Trent truly questioned his judgment at this point.

Phylicia knew that it was make or break time. The fact that Trent agreed to meet with her in the first place let her know that he still cared and that was all she needed working in her favor. She knew that he was outside because she was peeping out the window every two seconds since he had told her that he was coming over. She could see him sitting in his truck with his head on the steering wheel. If she wasn't in such a desperate position, she would have laughed at how pitiful he looked sitting out there as if he had the weight of the world on his shoulders. She understood that she had messed up royally, but she also knew how forgiving Trent could be and despite what he said, he loved her. That love is exactly what had brought him over to her apartment today and she was banking on how good it was between them before everything had gone down as crazy as it had.

Bracing himself as he stood outside Phylicia's door. Trent's mind was battling itself. His brain told him he should turn and leave. Retreat as if he had never come, but his heart needed to hear what she had to say. He'd given all he had to this woman he'd thought she was different. He couldn't take the cut-throat approach that he did with all the other woman he had encountered throughout his life and Phylicia knew he had a soft spot for her no matter how hard he tried to fight the feeling. But even his heart couldn't deny the fact she had played him and one of the main rules in the man code was men play women not the other way around. Somewhere along the line he had got the game messed up. Making up his mind with that last thought, he knew he didn't need Phylicia, he was better off without her. Turning away from her door to leave without ever knocking, he was surprised when he felt a light touch on the back of his arm.

Looking out the peephole watching Trent go through his inner struggle and then turn to leave, she knew that she was losing, which is why she quickly but quietly opened the door and touched his arm so he wouldn't just leave without giving her an opportunity to plead her case.

"You're not just going to leave without seeing me are you?"

Trent turned toward the sound of the voice he grew to love. There she stood, all five feet three inches of her. Clad in a red lace bra and panties, Trent felt himself rising to the occasion and he knew it was going to be a long night if he didn't make it out of there soon.

Trent let her pull him into her apartment and once she had him inside Phylicia knew she had won round one.

"I'm so glad you came over to talk to me." Phylicia said as she shut the door. "I would have hated for that whole club ordeal to be our last encounter."

Trent knew she wanted to seduce him, if what she had on wasn't enough, it was the sound of her voice, the look in her eyes and how she kept running her hands up and down his arms. Intentionally stepping just outside her reach, Trent was going to do his best to ensure that nothing happened this evening.

"You wanted to talk. So talk." He said as he sat on her black leather sofa. He had to hand it to her. She kept a nice place. When he'd first stepped in it had smelled like strawberries and cream. She'd always been a lover of strawberries. She was his lover. He reminisced about the times they used to entice each other with strawberries and cool whip and the mess they loved to make.

Sitting on her coffee table so she could face and be as close to him as possible, Phylicia was going to give this conversation her all.

"I officially want to apologize for the way things went down when we were together." Taking his hand into hers, she placed it on her breast over her heart.

"I called you over here because I want the opportunity for me to explain what happened and discuss the situation like rational adults to see if we believe this is something that is fixable."

Shaking his head, Trent removed his hand immediately when her hardened nipples grazed against his palm. There was no way that he was falling into her trap a second time. He didn't care how sexy she presented herself. Everything about Phylicia was poison wrapped up in a pretty package. Phylicia could feel the internal war he was waging. He was going to fight her every step of the way. She could feel it, but she had to make him see that she was the woman for him. Eyes slowly beginning to water she had to find a way to make him sympathize with her. There had to be a way.

"It's not fixable because I no longer trust you. There is nothing you can say to me that would make me take you back."

"But I love you." Phylicia felt the tears begin to slide down her face, "And despite what you think, I didn't intend for any of this to happen."

Now she had Trent's undivided attention because he couldn't believe her audacity.

"You didn't intend for exactly what to happen Phylicia?" His voice rose with each word he spoke to the point where Phylicia could tell she had struck a nerve, "The only thing you didn't intend to do was get caught. Now you standing here in your draws half naked begging me out here to talk to you expecting us to pick up where we left off. Do you think I'm stupid or something?" Trent angrily stood to his feet.

"No, I don't think you're stupid." Phylicia said as she slowly rose from the table.

"You must."

Debating whether to touch him or not, Phylicia honestly didn't know what to do. If she could turn back the hands of time she would, but she couldn't. She had to deal with the here and now and think fast. If she could get him into the bedroom, she knew she could work her voodoo on him and get him to stay.

"I'm not trying to play you for stupid. I really want to apologize for everything. I know you once loved me, and I know I messed up royally; you don't have to like me, but can you at the very least attempt to forgive me?" She leaned in and gently kissed his neck. While her hands found his belt buckle and undid his pants and slowly sank onto her knees. She knew exactly what she could do to make him happy. Placing his already hard dick into her mouth, she began to lick it like a lollipop, Trent didn't want to forgive her, but Phylicia was the special woman in his life. He'd once loved to hear the sound of her breathing as she slept in his arms every night. He would always have the memories of those moments. Not to mention that she was fine as hell. Then and now and there was no denying that he wanted her. Maybe hitting it one last time wouldn't hurt. Kodi did this type of thing all the time and he never seemed to regret anything. The more he thought about it the more he convinced himself. Leaning back on her sofa, he closed his eyes and allowed Phylicia to work her magic. He told himself he could spank that ass for the final time and be done with her and her scheming ways once and for all.

Chapter Five

Shia was so mad at Leigh, she could barely function. Ever since Leigh met Kodi, she'd been anything but reliable and it was beginning to irk Shia's nerves to no end. Once again, Shia had taken the dreaded bus ride up to New York because Leigh had said she wanted company, so being the awesome sister whom she was. Shia was here.

She was patiently waiting for Leigh to return to the apartment to let her in. The longer she sat there, the angrier she got. She couldn't believe that girl would leave her stranded out front of her building for over an hour.

Taking her cell out her purse, Shia scrolled her phone book trying to figure out whom she knew in New York that could rescue her. Since she didn't live here, there really was no one for her to call. Continuing to scroll, she came across Trent's name and paused. She didn't speak with him since the night they'd met in the club and that dumb woman ran up on them trying to start some drama. That was Shia's cue to leave. She hated drama and tried to avoid it at all costs, but if it couldn't be helped, she had no problem fuckin' a bitch up. It was what it was.

Deciding this was a good time for she and Trent to start over fresh, Shia hit the call button to dial his number. It was either that or stay outside waiting for Leigh's shady ass to show up and who knew when that would be.

Trent was hesitant about answering the unknown number that appeared on his phone.

"Yo." He said on the phone.

"Hi. It's Shia. You may not remember me...I met you in the club a few weeks ago. The one with the sister."

"I remember who you are. To what do I owe the pleasure of your call?"

"A sex-crazed sister who left me stranded on the sidewalk."

He laughed at her response. "Oh, so this call is more to do with you probably needing a ride, then it has to do with me. Am I right?"

For the second time since they had met, Shia was cold busted. Laughing a little herself, "If you don't mind picking up a straggler off the side of the road, I could really use some rescuing."

"You are far from a straggler. I should leave you out there the way you ran off at the club with no goodbye, glass slipper or anything."

"You were preoccupied with drama; I chose not to be bothered. Surely, you can understand that and understand how much I need you now."

"Ok, ok. I'll come get you. Text me the address and I'll be on my way."

Shia was elated when Trent pulled up in his pearl Escalade. She could finally stop looking homeless on the side of the street with all her bags.

Rolling down the driver's side window, Trent stuck his head out.

"Excuse me Ms, you seem like you could use a ride."

Shia smiled, "What gave it away? Surely not me sitting here on the curb with my bags?" she asked laughing.

Trent put the truck in park so that he could get out and help her with her luggage.

"Not at all," he responded.

"Good. I don't want to be looking all homely and what not."

"That would never happen; you're too beautiful for that."

Shia blushed at the compliment as they finished putting her bags in the truck and Trent held open the passenger door for her to get in.

"I really appreciate you coming to pick me up out of the blue like this. I have no idea where Leigh is. She was supposed to be here hours ago."

Looking over at her as he drove Trent thought it was really foul of her sister to leave her hanging on the street like that.

"It's not a problem at all. Luckily, I'm free all day today."

"Wonderful!" Shia said as she leaned her head back on the seat headrest and closed her eyes. She was tired. There hadn't been any rest to be found on the bus on the way up to New York because a baby would not stop screaming the whole way. And then sitting outside Leigh's apartment for two hours, she couldn't very well go to sleep on the street. Trent had no idea how much of a godsend he was to her.

Glancing at Shia, when his next question went unanswered, Trent noticed she had fallen asleep. Admiring the way her long lashes rested on her cheeks, his gaze wandered over the rest of her perfectly symmetrical features. She wasn't pretty in the conventional way; he would describe her more as cute. She had her waist-length hair pinned up, which accentuated her features. He loved the way her orange coat set off her caramel skin tone and the way her pouty lips were screaming kiss me as they slowly spread into a smile.

Quickly shifting his gaze up to her eyes, Trent saw that Shia was watching him beneath lowered eye lids.

"Like what you see?" she asked with a hint of a smile in her voice.

Trent refused to be embarrassed for being caught assessing her features.

"Absolutely." He responded.

Her cheeks suddenly flushed bright red.

"We're here." Trent said pulling his truck into the garage.

"Where is here?" Shia asked looking around.

"My condo."

Shia's heart began racing. He said that so nonchalantly. It actually made sense, where else did she think that he was going to take her. She wondered what he was thinking, or if he thought she was more like Leigh was and would be giving it up easy as her sister had done with Kodi. Realizing that she was overreacting over probably nothing, she forced herself to calm down as she got out the truck.

Trent wasn't too sure what to make of Shia's mood. She was silent since they had entered his home.

"Everything ok?" he asked her.

Sitting on Trent's plush couch Shia was in heaven, though slightly pissed that she still hadn't heard from Leigh.

"Everything would be cool if Leigh hit me back." She paused as she looked over at Trent, "Do you think you can ask Kodi if he has seen her? I'm beginning to worry."

"I suppose I could." Trent said picking up his phone to dial Kodi's number, "Does she normally pull disappearing acts like this?" he asked her as he listened to the phone ring on the other end.

"Not until she met Kodi. She's usually responsible, but since he's been in the picture home girl has taken leave of her senses.

"What it do T?" Kodi's crisp voice came through on the other end of the phone.

"You know how it is. Aye, I have Shia here and she's looking for her sister. You haven't seen her have you?"

"Nah man told you I'm trying to avoid that crazy bitch. She is no longer blessed enough to be in the god's presence."

"Aight man, be easy." Trent said as he hung up the phone. Looking over at Shia, her face was anxious as she waited to hear what he had to say.

"Kodi says he hasn't seen her."

Shia sat up on the couch. Now she was beginning to panic. Reaching into her purse for her cell, she attempted to dial Leigh's number again and she answered on the first ring.

"Shy, I am so sorry." She said in a rushed tone.

"Sorry! Where the hell have you been?" Shia was beyond angry. "You just left me stranded on the side of the fuckin' street!"

Leigh knew Shia was mad now because she rarely cursed. There was no way she could tell her that she was trailing Kodi all day and had discovered where his side chick stayed. She had yet to decide what she was going to do with that information, but first she had to deal with Shy.

"I got held up with some stuff. I'm so sorry. I'm on my way home now. Where are you? I hope you're not still sitting outside."

Shia couldn't believe Leigh's audacity. "It's too late to be concerned with my whereabouts now. I'm fine. Maybe I'll see you tomorrow when you have your priorities straight."

Leigh was shocked that Shia was really so upset that she wasn't coming back over to see her until the next day.

"I thought the point of you coming to my house was to hang out with me."

"That was the plan until your ass left me on the street for over two hours." Shia yelled into the receiver, "You need to stop being so selfish. Call me when you get it together." She said then turned off her cell. She was so irritated with Leigh. She couldn't understand what had gotten into her.

"So, I take it from what little I heard of that conversation that I should plan for an overnight guest?"

"I don't want to impose. If you don't mind taking me to a hotel, I should be fine." Looking over at Trent Shia was mortified. She had told her sister she wouldn't be coming over completely forgetting she had nowhere else to stay. Now she was really banking on Trent's hospitality and generosity.

"You may as well stay. You're already here, besides, I would enjoy the company."

Shia raised guarded eyes up at him, "You're not going to try to take advantage of me are you?"

Trent's lips parted into a smile, "Only if you want me too." He let his gaze wander over her full length.

Shia saw him eyeing her and laughed as she shook her head no. "I think I'll pass on that tonight, but if it isn't too much trouble, I would like to stay tonight and I promise to stay out of your way."

"You're not in my way. You're perfect." Trent said staring into her luminous brown eyes. Shia began to get aroused under his intense gaze. The chemistry between the two of them was crazy strong. She was going to have to watch out for Trent. He was dangerous for her mind, body, and spirit.

Chapter Six

It was two weeks since Leigh had left Shia sitting outside her apartment waiting for her. She was just glad that Shy was still speaking to her and had forgiven her for that whole little incident. She truly didn't do it intentionally. Kodi had cut her off and she wasn't having it. Who did he think he was? Treating her like she wasn't good enough to be a part of his world. No way was she going to tolerate this type of behavior from anyone.

After following Kodi for the last four weeks she was now able to find out about and track his Latina whore and their son and she could give two shits about either of them. All she knew was Kodi was meant to be her man by any means necessary.

Pulling her car into the parking lot, Leigh was ready to pounce. Entering the spa, she confirmed her appointment with the receptionist then sat in the waiting area for her name to be called. She knew what she was about to do was borderline foul, but she didn't care.

"Excuse me Ms." Leigh jumped a little when the receptionist gently touched her arm. She didn't realize she had zoned out.

"Ms. Rivera will see you now."

"Ok, thank you."

"No problem. Right this way please." The receptionist began to lead the way so Leigh quickly stood up to follow her down the hall.

The anticipation for her session was mounting. She was poised and ready to execute her carefully thought out plan. Entering into the back room where she would receive her massage, Leigh stopped short. She was stunned by how plain in appearance Ms. Rivera was up close and personal. The brief glimpses she'd had of her hadn't prepared her for what she saw. The way Kodi seemed like he couldn't get away from the woman, Leigh had expected someone more alluring. She'd expected someone that was worth being in competition with her for Kodi's affection. The woman who stood before her was shaped like a Cola bottle, but that was the only compliment Leigh could and would give to her. She stood about 5'8, had jet-black hair pulled back into a tight bun; slanted cat shaped eyes, a brown skin tint and was a perfect size six. To the world, Sherri Rivera was a beautiful exotic woman, to Leigh, she was barely scraping by in the looks department.

Sherri offered a warm welcoming smile to the woman as she entered.

"Hello, what would you like to get done today?" She said with a slight hint of an accent.

"A full-body massage please." Leigh answered sweetly. Stepping out of her clothes to lay on the massage table, she was glad that she was a faithful member of the gym around the corner from her apartment. Giving Kodi's baby mother an up close and personal view of her will defined toned body, she was more than amped and ready to put her plan into full effect.

"Your body looks nice. I can tell you work out. What gym do you go too?" Sherri asked.

"NY Sports Center." Leigh responded.

"Oh, really? My son's father works out there as well. He tells me it's a great place."

"It is." Leigh confirmed as Sherri began to knead the muscles in her tense back. Deciding it was now or never, she was about to punch a giant hole into Sherri's world when a light tap suddenly came at the door.

"I'm in a session right now." Sherri announced to the closed door without breaking the rhythm of her hands.

The door opened slightly as the receptionist poked her head through, "I hate to interrupt Ms. Rivera, but your son's father is out front and said he needs to speak with you right away."

"Ok, I'm coming." Sherri replied to the receptionist, "I apologize about this. I'll be right back." She said looking down at Leigh as she turned to walk out the door.

Leigh was barely listening to her. Kodi was here in the building? She had to see him. Jumping up off the table, she quickly downed her clothes and ran out to the lobby. Kodi and Sherri were easy to spot, appearing to be in a heated discussion.

Slowly walking in their direction, Leigh could get right up in Kodi's face because all of his attention was focused on Sherri.

"Hi baby, did you miss me?" Leigh asked as she squeezed in between him and Sherri placing a kiss on his lips attempting to slide her tongue in between them.

Kodi backed away from Leigh immediately with disgust in his eyes. Without looking back her way he turned and left Sherri's place of business.

Sherri looked at the woman she was massaging only minutes before as if she had lost her mind.

"Excuse me?" Sherri said to Leigh, "Why are you kissing on my man?"

"Trust me Mama; he ain't just your man." Leigh said silently daring her with her eyes to make a move.

Sherri jumped on the young woman knocking her to the floor and actively began to beat her face in blow by blow. Leigh kept trying to push Sherri off her, but Sherri wasn't having it. Fuck her and this job. Leigh had come in here to start some trouble and Sherri was determined to give her exactly what she came for.

"Get off me!" Leigh screamed as she unsuccessfully tried to dodge Sherri's punches.

"Dumb bitch! Is this why you came here? To start some shit, so why can't you get your ass off the floor?" Sherri screamed, pulling out a blade as she continued to bash Leigh's head in.

Those were the last words Leigh heard before she blacked out and the authorities arrived to cart Sherri off the jail.

* * * *

Waking up to the slow steady beat of a machine serenading her Leigh blinked fast trying to figure out where she was. Attempting to turn her head, she felt pain shoot through the whole left side of her face.

Sensing movement, Shia glanced up at the hospital bed from the chair she was sleeping in for the last day. She saw Leigh fidgeting around and immediately jumped up to assist her.

“Lei Lei, be careful. You don’t want to hurt yourself any more than you have to.”

"What happened to me?" Leigh managed to creak out.

"Gently brushing Leigh's wild hair off her face, Shia winced looking down at her. The left side of Leigh's face was sliced up, bitten & bruised so badly that a bystander would never believe they were identical twins.

"You got your ass beat."

Shia narrowed her eyes and shook her head at the comment their younger sister Remi had made. Leave it to her to break the news, “Gently.”

"Thanks Remi," Shia sarcastically began, "I'll take it from here."

Staring into Leigh's swollen eyes, Shia attempted to smile.

"That bad huh?" Leigh's raspy voice asked.

"Well," Shia began slowly, "Not technically that bad, but you look beaten up a little. What happened? You want to talk about it?

Leigh went to shake her head and then thought better of it when she felt the pain begin in her face.

"Umm, you gonna have to think of something because Ma is in the hall about to have a heart attack. Remi spotted her out there a few moments ago."

"Ma is here?" Leigh was shocked. It wasn't like their mother to drop everything and be by her bedside. She was selfish like that.

"Why?"

"What do you mean why? Because she's our mother."

"Shy, please don't take up for her. She gives selfish a whole other name."

"I'm not taking up for her. I'm stating the facts. She is “Our" mother."

"Spare me this conversation please. I just want to rest." Leigh said leaning into her pillows. She fell into her own thoughts, highly upset that Sherri put her into the hospital. This war was far from over. Sherri was going to get hers.

The hospital door suddenly banged open and Leigh could smell her perfume before she fully entered the room and spoke.

"Oh My God! My baby! Are you ok? Can you breathe? You look so terrible!"

Leigh's eyes rolled beneath closed lids. She wasn't in the mood to stomach her mother's irritating antics today.

“What happened to my baby?” Shia moved to the side as their mom almost trampled over her to get to the side of Leigh’s bed. Remi let out a disgusted sigh and left the room.

“Leigh, baby can you hear me?”

Shia almost laughed aloud as she observed Leigh, pretending to be asleep. She thought Leigh should pursue an acting career; she was definitely a comedic sight. Leigh displayed no signs of being sleepy only a few seconds before their mother burst through the door. Now she had her eyes shut. Her mouth was slightly open and she’d managed to be drooling. It was truly a pitiful sight to see.

“Ma, I think Leigh needs her rest right now. Why don’t you come back later, once she’s awake?”

Turning to gape at Shia as she spoke, their mother had a surprised look in her eyes.

“Shia, baby,” her mother began, while kissing the air above her forehead, “I didn’t see you standing there.”

Considering that she had practically knocked her over to get to Leigh's bed, Shia found that hard to believe and chose not to respond. That was their mother, a dramatic ex-beauty queen diva. Like Remi and Leigh, Shia harbored very strong negative feelings for their mother, but she tried to be the peacemaker between them all.

"Ok, baby," her mother said pushing past her in a transparent cloud of perfume, "I must go now, people to see, things to do. Muah!" Blowing air kisses as she strolled out the hospital room.

"Thank the Lord that crazy woman has gone away."

Shia turned back towards the bed to the sound of Leigh's voice and smiled at her.

"You are such a trip. How could you possibly not want to let our mother coddle you? It was a once in a lifetime opportunity and you missed out." Shia's voice oozed with sarcasm.

"Shy, please don't make me throw up. I'm too old at this point. I no longer need a mother. I have you and Remi, so I'm good. Speaking of which, where is Remi?"

"She stepped out when Ma sashayed in."

"I'm right here," Remi announced from the door, "I can't stand that lady. I left to get a breather."

"When can I get out of here? I'm ready to go."

"We can check you out whenever you're ready."

"Good," Leigh said shoving the covers off her, "Let's be out." She attempted to sit up and screamed in pain.

Shia and Remi both ran to her to help her sit up the best she could.

"What did that bitch do to me?"

"You have a few bruised ribs. You got beat up pretty badly. Your whole body will be sore for a while."

"Damn." Leigh mumbled.

Shia looked at her intensely. "You sure you don't want to talk about it."

"No Shy, I do not want to talk about it."

"I don't blame you boo." Remi chimed in, "I wouldn't want to talk about getting my ass beat either. I mean how embarrassing."

"Remi," Shia began in a stern tone, "Cut it out. You see that she's been through a lot, give it a rest."

"Ok, I won't say anything after I just say this one last thing," she paused for dramatic effect, "Leigh you look like shit." She said as she burst out laughing.

Shia closed her eyes and shook her head. Teenagers, especially seventeen-year olds what can you say, they will be who they are.

"Remi, you only got so much to say because you see me in this bed. Don't make me get up and hurt you."

Remi began to laugh even harder. "The same way you hurt whoever did this to you. Girl stop."

"Ok, enough. Both of you stop it. Remi, go out to the desk and check Leigh out. Leigh, let's get your clothes on so we can get out of here."

As Remi exited the room with no further commentary, Shia sighed a breath of relief. She hated when the two of them started to go at each other. They were so much alike that they honestly probably wouldn't be happy if they weren't fighting every other minute.

"If you knew I could leave, why did you tell Ma to come back later?"

Shia shrugged, "Just giving you time to get yourself together."

"Bless you Shy. God knew what he was doing when he teamed us up as twins."

Shia winked at Leigh and smiled. "Yeah, he did. Now you come on and get into these clothes."

Leigh tried her best not to flinch at the excruciating pain she was in as Shia helped her. Remi bounced in the room soon after the sisters successfully had Leigh ready to go.

"She's all checked out and your boo is in the hall waiting for us, so let's go before Ma returns."

Later that evening with Leigh back at her apartment resting comfortably, Shia was glad that Trent had stayed with her during this whole ordeal. Giving him a sheepish look, she was hesitant to begin talking.

"It would seem you've been inducted into the crazy ways of my family." She said with a smile.

Trent laughed, "It has been an interesting day." Feeling his phone vibrate he looked down to see Kodi's name across the screen.

"What's up?" Trent said into the phone.

"Man, that crazy bitch got Sherri arrested."

"Huh?" Trent was confused.

"Your girl's crazy ass sister, I told you that chick was loco. Now Sherri's in jail. I could kill that bitch."

"Yo man, hold up. Is that why ol' girl was in the hospital? She and Sherri got into it?"

"That crazy ho came up to Sherri's job and was there when I stopped by kissing on me and shit so I left. Next thing I know Sherri calling me from the police station saying she was arrested."

"Damn." Trent mumbled into the phone, "That is some crazy sh—"

"I need your help." Kodi said interrupting Trent.

"Yeah, whatever you need."

"You gotta stop seeing that crazy bitch sister because if you don't that will always give her crazy ass access to me."

"Don't worry about me and Shy. First, she's not like that and second your drama ain't got nothing to do with nothing. Anyway, what jail is Sherri in?"

"I thought you were my boy." Trent could already see how this was going to go. Kodi had a one-track mind.

"Yo, I've always been your boy and will always be your boy, but just because your hoes acting out of pocket don't think you can tell me what to do with my women."

"Whatever man. Sherri is good. Don't worry about us. I see it's come to bitches over everything suddenly."

Trent was shocked when he heard the phone click. Kodi, his boy had actually hung up on him. Trent shook his head. No wonder Kodi was always having woman problems, because he acted like one.

Shia was trying to make herself appear busy while she listened in on Trent's side of the phone call.

"Everything all good?"

"Yeah, everything's cool. That was just Kodi filling me in on his crazy day."

Shia eyed Trent suspiciously.

"I bet. Did he have something to do with Leigh ending up in the hospital?"

"I'm not getting in it. You want to know something then you should go and ask your sister."

Shia gave Trent the eye. She could tell that he knew exactly what had happened and just flat out wasn't going to tell her.

"I know you know." Trent began grinning, but didn't respond, "What do I have to do to get some answers out of you."

Trent slowly looked Shia up and down taking in all if her graceful curves, but still didn't utter a sound.

Looking into Trent's eyes, Shia melted under his gaze.

"Hey," Remi said as she entered the living room of the apartment. Lei Lei is sleep so I'm a run and get something to eat. You guys want anything?"

"No." They said in unison loath to break the trance bonding them together.

"Ummm, ok. Don't be trying to steal my food when I get back." Remi said as she exited the apartment.

Chapter Seven

"I'm so mad at you, I can't even think straight."

Sherri was pissed the fuck off. She was having the day from hell and the only thing saving Kodi's ass from her bashing his head in was because he was a cop, he'd been able to pull some strings and get her released from jail, but he was still going to feel her wrath. She lost her job due to today's debacle of a scene.

"Babe calm down. I got you out of jail didn't I?"

Sherri jumped up out of her chair and marched over to Kodi pointing her finger in his face.

"You're the reason I was locked up in the first place." Taking her finger, she mushed Kodi in the forehead. "Who was that girl? Some skank you fucking!" She spat out in anger.

"Nah, I barely even know that girl."

"You a black ass lie mothafucka!" Sherri yelled throwing punches at Kodi's body, "Why else would she come all the way to my job scheduling massages and start some shit?"

"Yo Sherri chill." Kodi said ducking her punches, "Don't be putting your hands on me." Kodi stood to his feet. He knew Sherri was mad, but if she couldn't keep her hands to herself, she was going to force him to restrain her psycho ass.

"And I'm not fucking her."

"Yeah, whatever." Sherri yelled narrowing her eyes, "If you ain't doing it now then you were doing it at some point. I'm not stupid Kodi. I'm tired of this shit with you. You always doing some grimy shit. Now I don't have a job!" She screamed as she picked up Kodi's car keys and launched them at his head. Smiling when they connected Sherri immediately put her hands up. She knew a fight was coming and Kodi didn't disappoint.

Charging her with everything in him Kodi was about to teach Sherri a lesson. Picking her up off the floor, he was careful to avoid her fists while she tried to pound him with body shots as he carried her to the bedroom. Roughly throwing her on the bed, he climbed up and straddled her. Looking down at Sherri tossing and turning trying to break out of his hands restraining her Kodi shook his head. Sherri was sexy as shit. He loved how her jet-black hair was fanned underneath her on the bed.

"Get up off of me!" She screeched squirming frantically trying to break free of Kodi's hold.

"I love you." He said bending his head down to kiss her. Sherri moved her face to the side so his lips were forced to contact her cheek. "You know I don't mean no harm."

Silent tears made their way down Sherri's face, "Then why you always gotta fuck them other women? Why can't I be enough for you?"

Kodi stared into her wet eyes, "You are enough." He said leaning down trying to kiss her again. And again, Sherri turned her head to the side making her cheek the only target for his lips.

Sherri's cell phone ringing made them both go still.

"Kodi please get off me so I can answer my phone."

"Say please, Daddy."

"Por favor Papi, pero todavia estoy enojada contigo." Sherri said, just to get Kodi off her so she could answer her phone. She would deal with him and his bullshit later.

Kodi smiled. He loved when she spoke in Spanish to him, even if she was still mad. Releasing her hands, he moved off of her so she could run for the phone.

"Hey chica, what you up too?"

Sherri was elated when she heard her home girl Phylicia's voice on the other end of the phone.

"Phylicia girl, where have you been all day? A bitch done messed around and got fired and arrested all in the same damn day."

"What in the world! Why were you fired? What happened?"

"Some skank Kodi has obviously been fucking came up to my job and had the nerve to schedule an appointment with me for a massage."

"Are you serious?" Phylicia whispered.

"Girl yes! But P, that's not even the worst of it. Kodi comes up there to tell me he let William go with his mother for two weeks to some event in California without discussing it with me first, so I didn't get a chance to say goodbye to my baby first."

"Kodi is crazy." Phylicia chimed in. Sherri continued speaking as if Phylicia hadn't uttered a word.

"I was so upset with him, but before I could get how I was feeling out, this skank bitch slides her way in between us and sticks her tongue down Kodi's throat."

"What?"

"Yes girl, in front of me and my whole damn job."

"Oh Lord, Sherri, so what did you do?" Phylicia already knew whatever happened it must have been bad.

"What do you think? I fucked that skank ho up right there at my job. Got fired on the spot and a bitch got arrested at the same damn time."

"Geez, all of this in one day?"

"Yes ma'am and I'm still pissed off. Kodi better sleep with one eye open."

"This is crazy, so do we know this ho?"

"I've never seen her before and she has a down south accent."

"Do you at least know her name?"

"Yeah, it's on the police report. Let me get it. Hold on."

Sherri put the phone down and ran into her room to retrieve the report from her purse. She saw Kodi sitting on the bed whispering into his phone as he smiled at her. Ignoring him, she ran back and picked up the phone.

"Leigh Richards. That's her name. I put that ass right in the hospital."

Phylicia breathed heavily on the other end of the phone, "Sherri. You gotta slow down girl. One more incident like this and they are going to give you real time. You gotta learn how to control your temper. If you gonna do something at least don't do it around video cameras and witnesses. Start covering your face or something. You keep going through this shit with Kodi. Jail is not sexy. Think before action next time."

"I know P, but COME ON! The bitch had it coming. She was asking for it."

"True, she was. Do you have any more information on this random skank?"

"No, but I'm going to get some and you're going to help me."

"How you bringing me into this?"

"Because as my lawyer, I'm sure you don't want to see your client in jail. Come on, P. Please do me this one favor. I know you can pull this girl's information."

"You know I have your back." Phylicia began to laugh. Sherri was crazy and she was just as crazy for agreeing to help her out.

"I'll see what I can find out. I'll call you back when I have something concrete."

"Thanks P." Sherri said hanging up the phone.

* * * *

Phylicia was trying her best to stay level headed about her and Trent's situation. She was determined to get her man back. Hopefully, he wouldn't hold the past against her forever.

Gently placing her sleeping baby girl Avionne in her crib Phylicia was anxious to conclude her research for Sherri. The two of them had gotten close when Phylicia had begun dating

Trent and the four of them would double date frequently at first. Since Phylicia was a lawyer she never hesitated when Sherri had her first assault charge against her and asked Phylicia to represent her. Ever since then they were thicker than blood sisters were, so Phylicia didn't take it kindly that some skank was trying to get at her friend's man.

Pulling out the envelope that the one of her private investigator friends had dropped off while she was trying to get Avionne to sleep, Phylicia was anxious to see what he had come up with. She'd told Sherri that she would get the info for her, but she wasn't going to risk being disbarred for doing something she had no just cause to be doing. That's why it paid to have friends who did everything under the sun in case you needed a favor. Opening the envelope she really wanted to know was what this scandalous heifer looked like.

Feeling like a kid at the candy store with a black card, Phylicia dove right in. She found out that Leigh Richards was a younger twin and had a younger sister. She lived in Brighton Beach, which wasn't too far from Coney Island in downtown Brooklyn. Moving all the tedious paperwork to the side, Phylicia finally had her hands on the photo and she couldn't believe what she saw. Throwing the picture down on her desk, she reached for the cordless.

"Hey Mami."

"Sherri, you will never guess what I received today." Not waiting for a response Phylicia continued, "I've met the girl you put in the hospital."

"Are you serious? Where do you know that ho from?"

"I met them several weeks ago at Club Haze."

"Them?"

"Yes, she has a twin."

Sherri sucked her teeth in disgust. "You mean to tell me that there are two of them?"

"Yes, the night I saw them. Leigh was with Kodi and her sister was with Trent."

"No shit! Bitch so why the fuck didn't you call me and tell me my man was there with some other woman?" Sherri exclaimed.

"I wasn't focusing on you and your stuff at the moment. I was trying to see what was up with Trent."

"Yeah, but you could have mentioned it or something. Damn. I should fuck you up. You supposed to let your girl know this type of thing."

Phylicia could tell Sherri was angry and hurt that she didn't mention it to her.

"I really didn't think about it."

"Yeah, cause your ass stuck on Trent. See if I tell you anything else." Sherri paused for a moment, "Damn P. That is so fucked up of you."

"Yo, my bad. Can we move on now?" Phylicia knew she made a mistake, but she wasn't going to be all broken up about it.

"Whatever. So these twin ho's think they're going to roll in and take our men. Hell no!" Sherri hissed. Angry at the situation. Leigh trying to get her man and Phylicia withholding information..

Phylicia hated to, but she had to take her feelings out at the moment and focus on the actual legal matters first.

"Unfortunately, you can't be running around doing anything to this girl. You have a court date and the state is going to prosecute you. We need to deal with that first. I'm going to recommend that you opt for a plea bargain because you are guilty. Admit guilt and I may be able to get you a lighter sentencing. What do you think?"

"I'll do whatever you think is best P as long as no jail time is involved."

"Ok. I'm going to try to work my magic, but you gotta stop putting people in the hospital. This is twice now. One more strike and you're out Mama."

"I know. I know. I will try to do better."

"You're GOING to do better because I'm adding anger management classes to your plea as an extra incentive."

“Cool, now can we get back to business. Where can we find these twins?”

“I have all the information. Come over my place and we’ll collaborate.”

“Be right over.” Sherri said hanging up the phone.

Chapter Eight

"Hey boo."

Leigh smiled at her reflection in the mirror when Shia came into the room and sat on the bed.

"Hey."

"What's the plan for today?"

"I don't know. Wanna go shopping?"

"We can do that. Been awhile since I've gone to anyone's store, but I have to be back by six. Trent and I have plans."

"Ohhh!" Leigh smirked throwing a pillow at Shia, "So that's why you come up to New York every weekend. And here I thought you were coming up to see me. My bad, what was I thinking?"

Shia's face broke into a huge grin. She was happy that Leigh was in a much better place than she was five weeks ago returning from the hospital. "Don't hate the playa, hate the game." She said throwing the pillow back at Shia.

"How are things with you and Kodi?"

Leigh continued to stare at herself in the mirror as she combed her hair.

"Ummm, nothing really to report. I haven't spoken to him since Sherri and I got into a fight. He's avoiding me."

"Who is Sherri?" Shia asked slowly. She didn't want to seem too forward. This was the first time Leigh had ever mentioned anything about the whole fight incident that had landed her in the hospital.

"Sherri," Leigh began as she combed her hair harder, "Is Kodi's son's mother. The one he couldn't stop fucking every other night when he was doing me."

"Oh."

"Yeah, I'm dealing with the whole thing my own way." Putting her comb on the dresser, she grabbed her purse, "You ready to go?" She asked turning to Shia.

"I am. Let's hit it." Shia said jumping up off the bed heading for the door.

* * * *

Shopping in New York was truly an experience, city life at its finest. There were people everywhere and Shia was thrilled to be a part of the hustle and bustle as well as being able to enjoy quality time with her sister for once. They needed some bonding time just the two of them without her running off to be with Trent.

"Damn today must be my lucky day. Two treats for one." Shia and Leigh groaned in disgust simultaneously and kept walking trying to avoid the train wreck of a boy walking their way.

"Baby girls you too pretty not to holla at your boy." A young Flava Flav look alike said running up in between them putting his arms around their shoulders.

Both stopped walking in unison.

"What are you, like twelve?" Leigh asked stepping away from his repulsive touch.

"We're enjoying our time together. Thanks, but no thanks." Shia said grabbing Leigh's wrist and walking away from the annoying guy.

"He was a hot mess!" Leigh said once they were a good distance away from him.

"You ain't never lied. Ewww." Shia coincided squinching up her face. "Ooo! Let's go in here."

"Really Shy, how many Coach bags does one person really need?"

"As many as I want. Come on." Shia said taking Leigh's hand and dragging her into the store.

"Lei, Lei look at this one. I love it." Shia said holding up a cream and metallic purse.

"Mmmhmn." Leigh hummed not paying attention to which purse Shia was referencing. She was too busy inspecting a wallet that must make a new home in her purse. It simply must.

"Well, well. Look who we have here. If it isn't the twin bitches from Maryland."

Leigh spun around towards the sound of the voice so fast Shia was surprised, she didn't give herself whiplash.

Phylicia and Sherri couldn't believe their luck. Randomly shopping with baby Avionne in tow, who did they see but the very two people they were secretly scheming on.

Leigh and Shia both narrowed their eyes at the two women staring back at them.

"What did you say?" Leigh took a step forward.

"I said and I quote 'Well, well. Look who we have here. If it isn't the twin bitches from Maryland'." Sherri repeated taking a step forward as well.

"Sherri." Phylicia said in a warning tone grabbing her arm. She didn't want Sherri getting too carried away. She had a case pending already and Phylicia had her baby out with them. She wanted to avoid drama if possible.

This was Sherri, Shia made a mental note to herself. She recognized the other woman Phylicia from the club that was trying to make a scene with Trent the first night she'd met him.

"Phylicia, nice to see you again." Shia offered up in the awkward silence trying to play nice by ignoring Sherri's ignorant comment,

"The pleasure is completely yours." Phylicia shot back.

"Still no class I see. Guess some things can't be taught. Come on Leigh, they're not worth our air space." Shia gently pulled on Leigh's sleeve to try to avoid an altercation, since she and Sherri appeared to be in a standoff never taking their eyes off one another.

"Just like you can't teach Trent to stay away from me that must eat you up at night."

"Not really, because he's eating me at night." Shia smirked, "Jealous?"

"Careful, we wouldn't want you to end up in the hospital like your sister." Sherri whispered through clinched teeth, "By the way," Sherri continued refocusing on Leigh, "Glad to see your face healed so nicely. Please don't risk getting it smashed in again."

Leigh took a quick step forward and punched Sherri in the mouth, smiling when she saw blood trickle out the split in her lip..

"You dirty bitch." Sherri lunged on Leigh and tackled her to the floor. Throwing punches all the way to the ground repeatedly pounding Leigh's face.

Security rushed in so fast Phylicia and Shia didn't have a chance to get involved even if they wanted too. Security detained Leigh and Sherri until the police came.

"I'm her lawyer." Phylicia announced while security was detaining the two women.

"That's nice ma'am; can you step to this side please?" The security guard asked Phylicia as he escorted Leigh and Sherri to the back.

Shia was mildly embarrassed. A small crowd had gathered from the commotion the women had caused. She was grateful when she saw police arriving, until she realized who was leading the pack.

"I'm here to pick up the individuals responsible for the disturbance."

Phylicia walked hurriedly over to Kodi.

"Kodi thank God it's you. Sherri got arrested again."

Kodi stopped in his tracks when Phylicia began speaking to him and focused his attention on her.

"What? Sherri's the one being detained?" He shook his head, "For what?"

"For fighting her sister." Phylicia pointed at Shia, "I swear where do you and Trent find these bottom dollar bitches?"

Shia ran over to where the two stood ready to pounce on Phylicia, only stopping when Kodi placed himself in between the two. "If a bottom dollar bitch has your so-called man, you obviously need to step your game up bitter ho. Trent told me all about your whorish ways. Seems like he dodged a bottom bitch to get a winner like myself to me."

"Ladies calm down. You two may as well go down to the station that's where my team will have to take Leigh and Sherri."

"This is all your fault." Shia hissed at Kodi, "You need to stay away from my sister."

Kodi laughed in Shia's face. "Trust me; I don't want anything to do with her. You need to tell your sister to stay away from me. Now if you'll excuse me ladies I have work to do." He said walking away from them leaving a team member between Phylicia and Shia so nothing popped off between the two. The rest of the team went to the back to collect the women and take them down to the station for processing.

Shia got the information of the station Leigh would be taken too and left the store. Pulling out her cell, she called Trent to tell him the story of everything that had gone down.

"Now you say what?" Trent asked after he'd come to pick Shia up from the store and headed down to the precinct.

"Yes. You heard me correctly on the phone. You and Kodi come with a lot of woman drama."

Trent opted not to say anything. Kodi was still acting like an emotional woman. Trent hadn't heard from him since Sherri got locked up the first time. And from the extra negative energy he was receiving from Shia, he could tell that Phylicia was beginning to wear on his nerves.

Riding in silence for a few minutes Trent could tell Shia was in deep thought.

"What's the deal with you and Phylicia anyway?"

Even though she had spoken softly, her voice boomed in the quiet truck. Trent didn't know exactly how to answer that question. What was his deal with Phylicia?

"What do you mean?" Trent asked stalling.

"Come on Trent," Shia gently touched his arm, "Seriously. Something's up."

Trent refused to look at her as he continued to drive. Shia wasn't a fool and he didn't want to offend her by lying to her.

"Honestly, nothing is up now. I used to love her. Part of me still does, but I can't be with her. She's no good for me. She just hasn't come to grips with that yet, but she will. Eventually."

"Are you still sleeping with her?"

Trent didn't want to answer her question because though he and Shia were dating, they still hadn't had sex yet though they dabbled in oral sex a lot. She'd told him she was waiting for marriage first. She was a wholesome kind of woman, which was one of the things he admired about her, even if it was driving him crazy that she wouldn't give him any.

"Sometimes."

Shia grew quiet and was shocked by Trent's honesty.

Trent glanced at her before pulling into a parking spot at the precinct.

"You're upset now?" He asked.

"Yes and no." Shia said looking him directly in his eyes. "I asked the question, so I have to handle the answer. At least you were being honest." She said opening the truck door as she got out and headed into the precinct.

Leigh was sitting on a bench in the lobby when they walked in.

"Hey Lei Lei, you ok?" Shia asked sitting down next to her twin and embracing her.

"I'm ok Shy." Leigh replied as Trent came up to stand in front of them. "The store isn't pressing charges; they just ban us from coming back."

"Oh goodness, how will Coach ever live without us?" Shia said. Leigh cracked a smile at that.

"You're silly."

"I know and I love you. The good thing is you don't have any charges."

"Yeah, I guess." Leigh was very mellow.

"So you ready to go?' Shia asked standing up.

"Not quite." Leigh responded refusing to stand up.

"What else do you need to do?"

"Talk to Kodi." Leigh replied sheepishly.

Trent shook his head at her response, but opted out of saying anything.

"Yo T what's good?" Kodi spoke to Trent when he came out to the lobby and gave Trent dap.

Trent returned the gesture and let bygones be bygones.

"Nothing. Just seeing what's going on."

"Yeah, this shit is crazy." Kodi said tipping his head toward Leigh.

"Trent, what are you doing here?"

Trent froze at the sound of Phylicia's voice. When Phylicia and Sherri saw Shia and Leigh, they all stopped short.

If the situation hadn't been so heinous, Trent would have laughed. He and Kodi exchanged looks of disbelief. What were the odds of a standoff like this happening with both caught between the women they were dating and women they had slept with? The two men stood between the four women and no one was saying anything. The women all continued to glare at one another.

"I'm here with Shia to pick up Leigh." Trent said breaking the silence.

Phylicia narrowed her eyes at Shia, but didn't say anything. She knew where Trent would be spending his night and that's all that mattered.

"Kodi, I need to speak with you." Leigh suddenly blurted out.

"No Mami, you don't. Know your place." Sherri fired back at Leigh.

Kodi laughed and escorted Sherri out giving Trent more dap before he left. "I'll holla later T."

"Aight bet."

When the trio strolled out the building, Trent looked back at Shia and Leigh.

"You two ready?"

"I think so." Shia tickled under Lei's chin, "You ready kiddo?"

"Yeah, whatever. Let's go."

Shia could tell that Leigh's feelings were hurt, but what could she do. Leigh had to be strong enough to deal with reality. Kodi didn't want her; she had to find it in herself to move on.

Chapter Nine

Ever since Trent had disclosed to Shia that he was still having sex with Phylicia, she was rethinking her whole wait until marriage theory. She wanted Trent only dealing with her. She couldn't understand how after everything Phylicia had done to him that he would still sleep with her.

Shia began packing her clothes; she was headed to New York again for the weekend.

"Shia baby, when do I get to meet this friend of yours?" Shia cringed at the sound of her mother's voice.

"Ma, I'm not sure what you mean." Shia replied playing dumb.

Her mother came into her room and sat on her bed. Shia packed faster to minimize their conversation time.

"Come on Shy, you can confide in me. I know you're not only going up to visit Leigh at school all the time."

"I really am Ma. There's nothing to tell." Shia looked at her, "Really." She added for emphasis.

"Mom!" Remi yelled from down the stairs. "Can I go over to Malia's house? Dad told me to ask you."

Shia's mother rose from the bed, "Remi, what did I tell you about yelling through the house?" Glancing back at Shia before she left, her mother conceded defeat. "Ok Shy, even though you don't want to tell me about your friend, enjoy your trip. I have to go see what your sister has on before she leaves the house. Lordie that child."

Shia breathed a sigh of relief when her mother finally exited her room leaving a distinct scent of Marc Jacobs Daisy in her wake.

* * * *

Walking into Leigh's apartment Shia was surprised to hear the sound of a child playing in the back room. After Leigh had left her stranded on the street that one time, Shia had demanded a key.

"Lei Lei." Shia yelled into the apartment.

"Shy!" Leigh came running into the living room to greet her sister, "I didn't expect you till later."

"I was anxious to get out of Maryland. Ma was trippin'."

Leigh sighed, "Isn't she always?"

Dropping her bags in the living room, Shia went to investigate.

"I heard a child. You babysitting for someone?" She asked Leigh as she walked toward the backroom where she thought she heard the child playing.

"Not exactly babysitting." Leigh said right on Shia's heels.

Opening the bedroom door Shia was shocked to see a cute little boy roughly around the age of three sitting in the middle of the floor playing with toys.

"So what do you call it?" Shia asked leaning her body against the doorframe of the room.

"Shy, I think I'm in big trouble this time."

A bad feeling swept over Shia's body. She stood up straight giving Leigh her undivided attention.

"What did you do? Whose child is this?"

Leigh lowered her head, "Kodi's."

Shia was shocked. "Kodi let you babysit his son? I didn't know you two were cool again."

"Well, not exactly."

"Leigh." Shia said in a stern tone. She knew whatever her twin had done this time, there was going to be hell to pay for it.

Closing the little boy back in the bedroom Leigh was trying to think of a good way to explain.

"Does Kodi know his son is here?"

"Yes."

“Ok, so I’m confused. If he knows he’s here, why do you think you did something bad?”

“Because I took him before Kodi knew I took him.”

Shia closed her eyes and shook her head. Leigh was always doing crazy stuff without thinking anything through now Kodi was going to come here and probably try to kill her.

“Why would you take his child?”

“To force him to meet with me.”

“Leigh, Kodi is a douche bag. You need to let him go.”

“I tried and I can’t.”

“Why be with a man who doesn’t want you? You’re embarrassing yourself and risking going to jail. You can’t just take people’s freakin’ children Leigh. Where did you take him from anyway?”

“We’ll see." Leigh began to fidgit and Shia began to get worried.

"What?" She asked looking at her sister anxiously.

"I knew Kodi was going to take him to the park because," Leigh broke off before she told her sister that she was following Kodi rather than going to her classes. "Well it doesn't matter why I knew, and Kodi took a call and walked out of sight and I lured him over with candy." “Oh my god. This is worse than I thought." Shia was trying her best to stay calm, "Leigh, what in the world. You cannot kidnap people's children? That is a felony. Do you really think Kodi is worth going to jail over?”

Shia wanted to scream on her sister, but Trent calling her brought her interrogation of Leigh to a halt.

“Hello.” She said into her cell.

“Please tell me that your sister didn’t take William."Shia sighed as she shook her head, “I wish I could say that, but I can’t.”

“I’m on my way over there, be on the lookout for me.

“Ok.” Shia said as they ended the call.

* * * *

"I'm going to kill that bitch." Kodi could barely contain his rage.

Trent had just hung up with Shia and Kodi was sitting in his truck next to him.

"Let me go up first and see what I can do. I honestly think she just did this so you would have to talk to her."

"Nah, I'm going right up when we get there. You see T. Shit like this is why she's no longer blessed to be in the god's presence. Psycho bitch."

Trent couldn't understand how Kodi was maintaining. Even in Kodi's angry state, he was going easy on Leigh because he could have the whole force down here ready to lock her up.

Trent texted Shia to let her know he arrived and was on his way up.

Shia opened Leigh's apartment door for Trent and turned pale when she saw Kodi walking behind him.

Oh shoot. Shia thought as she let them in.

"Daddy!" The little boy squealed with happiness when he saw Kodi enter.

Kodi instantly bent down, swooped the little boy up into his arms, and hugged him tight.

"Where's Leigh?" Trent whispered to Shia while Kodi reconnected with his son.

"She's in the back. She didn't know Kodi was coming with you."

"T can you watch William for a minute. I gotta handle something first."

Kodi looked lethal as he headed to the back room.

"He's not going to kill Leigh is he?"

Trent hoped not, but who knows what a parent does when an unauthorized person takes your child. He could only imagine.

"Nah. He and Leigh just need to handle their business once and for all." He answered in a calm tone, trying to reassure Shia and himself.

When Kodi reached the back room, Leigh was ready for him. She'd heard William scream Daddy.

"Are you fucking crazy?" Kodi got right in Leigh's face and smacked her. "Do you know what I could do to you?" He asked in a menacing voice as he grabbed her wrist and began applying pressure. Leigh screamed out in pain as it felt like her wrist was about to break.

"Kodi please," she cried as her cheek throbbed from his smack, "I was never going to hurt him; it was the only way to get you here to talk to me."

"If stealing my son is the only way to get me to talk to you. It's obvious I have nothing to say to you. Know your place. A fuck was a fuck. That's it and it wasn't even good, feel me."

"How can you say that?" She cried.

"You buggin', acting like a clown right now. Hasn't Sherri beat your ass enough. You lucky I don't kill you for this shit. Come around me or my son again and I'll have you wishing you were dead." Kodi hissed letting her wrist go.

"But I love you." Leigh said as she rubbed her wrist where Kodi's fingers left a visible print.

"Kill yourself." Kodi spat at her exiting the room.

* * * *

Kodi answered his phone on the first ring. "You didn't tell me that bitch took William!" Sherri screamed into the phone.

"I have him." Kodi could squeeze into the conversation in the middle of Sherri's rant.

"Oh thank God! Is he okay?"

"Yeah, he's good. He's in the back of T's truck knocked out. How did you know William was missing?"

Sherri knew she wasn't supposed to know but she didn't care.

"Because Phylicia's friend is a private investigator and has been tailing her for the last couple of weeks. He told Phylicia who called Trent and now I'm speaking with you. You wait until I see that bitch. I'm a catch another muthafuckin' case."

"Sherri, it's handled, I took care of it."

"You took care of it!" Sherri screamed. "You're the reason it happened! If you learn to keep your fuckin' dick to yourself this never would have gone down."

"Yo chill. I'm a hit you back."

"Whatever Kodi, this ain't over! Tell that bitch she betta watch her step!" Was what Kodi heard as he disconnected Sherri's call.

Trent laughed. "You keep messing with these crazy women. Better watch *your* back son."

* * * *

"This some crazy shit. I'm a get disbarred if I keep fooling with you." Phylicia said.

"Mami you good, chill out. You just looking out for your girl. Cause this bitch crazy if she thinks I'm a just let her kidnap my son and walk away from that shit. Not happening."

Phylicia never understood how she let Sherri talk her into half the mess she ended up in. They were sitting under the steps staking out Leigh's apartment waiting for her to return home from school.

"Aye, ain't that that bitch right there?" Sherri whispered.

Phylicia glanced down the sidewalk and sure enough, Leigh was walking in their direction.

"Yeah that's her."

"Game on." Sherri said slowly creeping out from under the steps.

Jamming to her iPod as she walked up the street to her apartment building, Leigh was caught off guard when Sherri jumped in front of her seemingly from out of nowhere.

"You stealing babies now bitch!" Sherri punched Leigh in the side of her neck. The impact almost made Leigh blackout.

Leigh never had a chance due to the surprise attack. Sherri literally jumped on her back and crushed Leigh blow by blow until she fell to the ground.

"Hey, that's enough!" Phylicia said in a loud whisper. "She lying on the sidewalk barely breathing. You don't want to kill the girl."

Sherri raised her foot and kicked Leigh in the head as her final touch. "Dumb bitch. I bet she'll think twice before she steals anyone else's baby." She said before she and Phylicia turned and left Leigh on the sidewalk in front of her apartment building gasping for air.

Chapter Ten

Shia couldn't understand where the time had gone. It was months since she had met Trent, months since the Coach Store and Leigh stealing Kodi's son for an afternoon and was in the hospital after her second fight incident. As much as Shia wanted to worry about what was going on with Leigh now, she couldn't. She had her own life to follow through on, which brought her to her and Trent's situation.

Something was up with him. Even though they had only been dating for a few months she could tell things weren't the same; where he had once answered the phone, now she received his voicemail and texts instead. She needed and wanted answers immediately, which is why she once again took the four-hour journey to New York to get some of them. Shia had taken the liberty of inviting Trent over to Leigh's apartment to talk. Leigh had gone out to ensure Shia had privacy to handle her business.

Making sure she was looking cute Shia had gone the more casual route rocking dark-blue stretch jeans, a black low vee cut halter and a pair of black peep toe flats. Wearing her hair down, tonight she opted to part it down the middle with soft waves flowing throughout. She knew she looked good, now it was a matter of seeing where Trent's head was these days.

As if right on cue a knock came at the door. Shia gave a quick glance into the hall mirror and answered the door. There stood Trent. He was so handsome to Shia, but that didn't mean he didn't have to explain himself.

"Hey beautiful," he said placing a soft kiss on her forehead as he entered, "How are you?"

Trent was dreading tonight. He just wanted to get the whole ordeal over with; so consumed in his thoughts, he barely heard Shia ask him how he was doing.

"I'm good. What about you?"

Slowly closing the door behind him, Shia could tell that he was distracted.

"I've had better days." He said, "But you called me over here to discuss something so what's on your mind?"

"Well, have a seat first we can ease into it. We don't just have to go all in."

Sitting in the recliner next to the sofa, Trent waited for Shia to have a seat before speaking.

"I'd rather we jump right in. I have an appointment in about an hour to get to."

"Oh," Shia said slowly. Now she felt rushed as if he had something more important he'd rather be doing than talking to her.

"There's something that we need to talk about."

Shia could already tell by his tone that she wasn't going to like anything he was about to say.

"Do I really want to hear this?" she asked him.

"Probably not." Trent was feeling bad about the situation ever since it had happened. He just wanted to get it off his chest and be done with it. Lowering his head into his hands, he rubbed his forehead not believing his own stupidity.

"Phylicia's pregnant."

"Huh?" Shia was confused.

"Yeah."

"Wait, I'm trying to understand what's going on here." Shia had expected him to say work was keeping him busy or something. Not Phylicia was keeping him busy.

"Phylicia? Are you sure it's yours this time?"

Trent felt foolish now.

"Pretty sure."

"Amazing." Shia whispered as she stood up, "You can leave now. I no longer have a use for you."

"You don't want to talk about it? It was a small mistake." Trent tried to explain as he stood as well.

"You call a pregnancy a small mistake?" Shia couldn't believe the audacity of men, "I'm not even mad, since we're only dating and not officially together, but I am disappointed in you and your actions. Right now, you need to focus on what's going on in your life now. Not me."

Gently guiding Trent to the door without saying anything else, Shia let him out. She'd be lying if she said she wasn't sad. She'd really wanted things to work with Trent, but she'd be damned if she ended up in someone else's mess.

Her cell ringing abruptly broke her thoughts of self-pity. Grabbing it off the coffee table she glanced at the unrecognizable number and placed it back down pressing the ignore button. The phone immediately began to ring again.

"Hello?" she answered timidly on the second ring, apprehensive about who could be on the other end.

"Shy, you gotta come home now." Barely able to recognize Remi's voice over the static in the phone line, Shia heard the urgency in her tone.

"Remi, what's wrong?"

And that's when Shia heard it, the tears were apparent as Remi continued to speak.

"Something terrible has happened. You just have to come home right now. You have to. I need you. I don't know what to do." Shia's eyes began to tear up from all the hurt she could feel in Remi's voice.

"Ok, ok baby sis, slow down. Try to tell me what's wrong."

"Mommy and Daddy." Remi trailed off.

"Mommy and Daddy what?" Shia's heart began to beat at an ungodly speed. She began taking slow breaths trying her best not to panic as she listened to the silent line waiting for Remi to say something.

"Remi!" Shia shouted into the phone, "Mommy and Daddy what?" After another minute of a silent pause, Shia heard Remi's small whisper.

"Are dead."

Shia closed her eyes and slid to the floor. The tears that had watered her eyes a few moments earlier fell leaving little wet circles on the carpet.

"It can't be." She whispered to an empty receiver or maybe God because Remi had hung up.

* * * *

The funeral service for their parents was devastating to Shia. She was all torn up and her sisters were a lot more chill than she was. They were sitting next to her in the service whispering and giggling the whole time. Nothing could have prepared her for this. Just a week ago, she was trying to figure out where her relationship with Trent was going; now she was trying to figure out what was going to be made of her life. Her parent's house was half burned to the ground. Remi was now legally an orphan since she wasn't of age and Shia had no idea where they were going to live. Suddenly, she was thrust into the role of parent and caregiver. The only plus side to her parent's death was that they had left them each a large sum of money in their insurance policies, to which Shia was grateful.

"Will you two cut the games out? We are at our parent's funeral for goodness sake." Shia told Leigh and Remi in a stern tone. She hated the fact that they made her be the adult out of the group.

"Seriously Shia be easy aight. We know where we are." Leigh said turning to her with an attitude.

"Well then act like it."

"You can cut the act okay. Our parents are gone now; we don't need you stepping in trying to be our mother. We already had one of those and you see how that worked out."

"You would think you two didn't care by the way you're behaving, and as far as Remi is concerned, I am her mother now. Are you going to step in and be it?" Shia said shaking her head in disgust at the two of them.

"No and you ain't my damn mother, just remember that." Leigh mumbled.

"Whatever." Shia said rolling her eyes.

Chapter Eleven

Two Years later - January 29, 2007

"Two, four, six, eight, who does he appreciate? Not my ass that's for sure." Shia was definitely having a moment. She and Trent were on the outs for about the thousandth time since they had officially begun dating a year ago, and she was plain sick of it.

Hanging up in exasperation as his cell went straight to voicemail for the third time that night, Shia was heated. She just knew he was still at his baby momma house doing only God knows what with her. He'd said he was going to stop by, see his daughter, and then come over. Her gaze drifted towards the grandfather clock as the hour chimed eleven, shifting her eyes toward the dining room table, which was perfectly set for two; she felt the disappointment overwhelming her body. The wax dripping down the lit candles mirrored the tears sliding down her face and she knew she'd had enough.

Taking the stairs two at a time, Shia entered her room and began removing all of Trent's clothes. She didn't care anymore. Grabbing as many clothes as she could she ran down the stairs, opened the front door, and threw his stuff outside. She couldn't do this anymore. Trent couldn't seem to be the man she needed him to be. It took her eight trips, but she was finally able to have all of his clothes out on the lawn.

Back in the kitchen she walked over to the drawer that had all of her tools and pulled brand new locks that she had bought ages ago on sale in case she ever needed to change her locks. Unscrewing the screws one by one to the knob, she worked quickly as she did what she needed to do. Stepping back when she was done to admire her handy work, she smiled at the new locks now in place and shut the door, locking it behind her.

Turning off the kitchen light after cleaning the dinner, she had made to celebrate her and Trent's one-year anniversary, Shia knew that she was done with him. She was tired of the same foolery day in and day out that Trent fed her on a platter. Slowly walking up the stairs and into her candlelit bedroom, fresh tears poured down her face. Blowing out each candle was extremely difficult when one couldn't catch their breath in between the tears. As she walked into the bathroom to start her bath water, she poured scented bubble bath into her water leaving the lights off to watch the flame of the few candles she left lit dance along the wall to their own whimsical beat. Undressing in the hollowing silence, Shia entered the lavender scented tub allowing the water to continue to run over her discontented body. For the life of her, she couldn't understand how she had gotten to this point with Trent. Everything started so heavenly with the two of them that she thought as she replayed the day she and Trent had reunited in her mind.

* * * *

January 29, 2006 - The Sisters

Shia was upset. This was the third time she had to fill up her gas tank this week and it was only Friday. Her twin sister Leigh borrowed her car all the time and always left her tank on "E." Shaking her head in disgust she watched as the numbers kept rising; it cost her fifty-three dollars to feed her sleek black Nissan Altima baby. It was getting more and more expensive to take care of her car. She was seriously contemplating getting a bicycle to ride around town.

"You think since you borrow my car so much or need a ride some place that you can start filling my tank back up or providing a sister with some gas money? Geez!" Shia said getting back into the car. "Leigh, you have to do better. You are costing me a fortune. I can't afford you."

"Oh, my bad. You know I be strapped for cash. When I have some extra, I'll pass it your way."

Shaking her head, Shia knew what that meant. She would never see any money. She truly could not understand how she and Leigh could be identical on the outside and completely different on the inside. Cause Leigh was a mess. Born three minutes behind Shia, she took being younger to the extreme. She didn't take responsibility for anything. A college dropout, hopping from one job to the next, Leigh only believed in having a good time. To her the world was one big party and she was going to dance her way through life.

"Shy, don't be that way. I promise ok." Leigh began pouting her full lips and Shia had to laugh. It was like looking into a mirror. Leigh only called her Shy when she was trying to get her way and Shia couldn't help it, of course she had a soft spot for her twin and Leigh knew it. Their bond was strong.

"Aight little girl I hear you, but seriously," Shia pulled down her shades to give Leigh the look, "You have got to get it together. We're too old for you to be acting like this."

"Shy, you're old enough for both of us. I just want to have fun."

Shia rolled her eyes behind her shades as she drove; it was times like this that she missed having their parents around. Ever since their parents was murdered the previous year, she felt as if both of her siblings were stuck in that time frame, refusing to grow up and she was sick of it. Sometimes she wished that just for a space in time, her parents could be alive again and she could be the carefree person that she used to be. A tear escaped the corner of her eye and she really wished she could talk to her Dad. She had always been a Daddy's girl. She needed his comfort right this minute. Just to hear him say, "It will all be ok, baby girl." She would give up the rest of her life for that one moment.

"What's wrong with you?"

Leigh's question abruptly brought Shia out of her zombielike state.

"Missing Daddy."

Leigh looked at Shia with the tears still present in her eyes and sadly shook her head. Shia had always been the softy out of the three siblings. Sometimes Leigh honestly thought she and Remi were more like twins and Shia was the third wheel.

"You always missing Daddy. It's over and done, He and Mommy left us. We didn't leave them. As far as I'm concerned, "F" em." Leigh said as she watched people walking across the street while she and Shia were waiting for the light to turn green.

"I'm entitled to miss Daddy. I know what Mommy did was wrong, but Daddy isn't really to blame for that. I still miss the good times and he was always good to us."

That last comment snapped Leigh's attention away from the scurrying pedestrians.

"What do you mean good to us?" Her voice rose slightly. "How can you sit over there and say that with a straight face?" Leigh rolled her eyes at Shia's audacity.

"Leigh, they were good to us. They raised us to the best of their ability."

"You are so delusional. Good parents don't do what they did and you know it. They were selfish. Plain and simple."

Shia kept quiet. She knew there was no point in arguing with Leigh. Their parents were a touchy subject for her two sisters, so she dropped the topic entirely.

Pulling into the garage at their house, or Shia should say, her house that Leigh and Remi roomed in, she noticed that Leigh was quiet since their parents was mentioned and being quiet was definitely not the norm for Leigh's character.

"Hey, you ok?" Shia asked Leigh as they exited the car.

"Yeah, I'm cool." She replied. Her demeanor was completely nonchalant.

"You sure?"

"Shy, I'm good ok." Leigh said going into the house ahead of Shia.

Closing the garage door, Shia followed Leigh's entry at a slower pace, not in a hurry to deal with her sister's "Bipolar" attitude.

"Hola Mamacita!" Shia instantly smiled as Remi greeted her. Shia shook her head as she took in Remi's appearance. Standing tall at 5'10" with cocoa skin, her hair was shaved on one side, pink, purple and blue on the other. She had her lip, nose, eyebrow and ten ear piercings, a dog collar around her neck, chain around her waist that linked back to the dog collar, a sundress and flip flops with two tattoos showing, one that wrapped all the way down her leg and one on her foot. Shia came to the conclusion right then that there was no one in the world like Remi. No one.

"Taking up Spanish now?" Shia asked Remi as she set her things on the kitchen counter.

"Or something. What's wrong with Leigh?" Remi asked as she turned back to the dinner she was preparing. "She came in without saying anything and went straight upstairs."

Peeping over Remi's shoulder to see what she had sizzling on the stove, Shia was happy to see the ingredients for fajitas being sautéed. Resting her head on the back of Remi's shoulder, she answered her question cautiously.

"I mentioned Daddy while we were out and I'm thinking it got to her."

"Oh, so why are you leaning on my shoulder?"

Shia smiled. That was just like Remi. If she didn't like where a conversation was headed, she avoided it altogether.

Lifting her head off her shoulder, Shia gently mushed Remi in the back of her head.

"Excuse me for trying to bond with my sister. Go on and be Cinderella then. I expect my dinner at seven."

Remi laughed, "Sorry sis. I have a date coming over. No fajitas for you."

"What! You didn't tell me that you were having company this evening. The house is a mess and what if I had someone coming over?"

Remi looked at Shia as if she had two heads, "Shy, you never have company. When's the last time you had some testosterone to entertain?"

"That's not the point." Shia responded in an exasperated tone. "You still need to make me aware if you plan on entertaining company."

Cutting off the stove burner, Remi turned and gave Shia her complete attention. "Shy, it was not my intention not to tell you. Honestly, I didn't think about it." Walking up to Shia to give her a hug, Remi continued, "You are more than welcome to stay and have dinner with us. I'll have my date bring a friend along." She paused as she gave Shia a sly look, "Cause you need someone to brush the cobwebs off that thing. Been too long girlfriend, you need to release all that stress because you too uptight." She laughed.

Shia was mildly offended, "I am not uptight." She laughed while plucking Remi in the neck.

Remi gave Shia the, "Girl please" look.

"Ok, ok," Shia said still laughing, "Maybe I do need some male attention. But I don't need you calling me out on it. Now moving on to more pressing matters, can you go check on Leigh? She's more receptive to you." Hearing Remi suck her teeth and mumble under her breath, Shia knew she didn't want to tackle the hellion known as Leigh, but neither did she.

Remi pouted her lips, "Shy; I don't feel like dealing with old Mommy and Daddy drama right now. Plus my date will be here soon. Speaking of which, you may want to freshen up since I'm going to ask him to bring a friend."

"Girl please. There is nothing wrong with the way I look, nothing at all."

"Well, I'm not no Tyra or anything giving Top Model makeovers, but I'm just saying you may want to run a comb through your hair or something."

"Forget you Remi." Shia laughed, patting her bun that was held in place by a pencil with flyaway pieces hanging down her back, not the least bit offended, "I'm a go hop a shower real fast and curl my hair since my baby sis seems to think I will offend some man's sensibilities."

"There is a God." Shia laughed as Remi's statement followed her out the kitchen.

Along Came Trent

"Dinner was so good, never had fajitas that tasted quite like those before."

Shia glanced up as Khalil made his comment. He was Remi's date and she couldn't stand him. Everything about him was a no, no for her in a man and to make matters worse; she didn't like the way he treated Remi. Trent, Khalil's friend, on the other hand was very charming and a blast from the past. Shia couldn't believe the circumstances that had brought them together for a second time. She wasn't sure if these were better or worse circumstances, however. Trent was even more handsome and charismatic than she remembered him being. He oozed sex and she had to have him. He smiled suddenly and as Shia's eyes collided with his, it became painfully obvious that Trent had caught her staring at his month. Blushing profusely, Shia wanted her chair to swallow her up whole. She was so embarrassed. Dropping her gaze down to the floor, she was happy when she noticed the two men preparing to leave before she could further humiliate herself.

"Hey?"

Shia looked up at the sound of Trent's voice.

"Hey." She shyly responded.

"Will you walk out with me?"

Shooting a quick unsure glance at Remi, Shia didn't know what to do and Remi was no help. She and Khalil disappeared just that fast.

"Sure, I'll walk you outside." She mumbled.

Trent laughed as he followed her out the door. “Don’t sound so excited about it.”

Shia smiled at that. She had said it as if he had just invited her to a funeral.

“Sorry,” she responded, “I’m not too good at this awkward, forced, small talk conversation thing.”

“You weren’t this standoffish when we first met. What’s changed since then?

A lot. She thought to herself. Mainly, her parents being killed. She was a completely different person than the carefree girl he had met years ago.

“Um.”

“Hard question huh?”

Shia was becoming mildly offended. It seemed as if he was continually laughing at her expense.

Taking a brief pause to get her thoughts together, she stopped walking and responded matter-of-factly, “Actually, no it was not a hard question. I’m just different is all.”

“Baby girl, I wasn’t trying to offend you. I was only asking a question.” Trent hurriedly said sensing that he had somehow pissed her off.

“I’m not your baby,” Shia quickly replied with a slight attitude.

Trent turned to gently grasp Shia by the shoulders, “Hey,” he said tipping her chin up, “I am not a bad guy. I really was only asking you a question.”

* * * *

Shia snorted from the memory as her mind and body returned to a freezing reality, realizing she had dozed off and her bath water was now cold. “He’s not a bad guy.” Shaking her head at those hollow words Trent had spoken to her the night they were reunited, she sighed as she exited the bath. Seeing the red light blinking on her blackberry indicating she had a new message as she reentered her room Shia shook her head in anticipation of what was sure to come. Retrieving her phone she saw that she had missed two of Trent's phone calls and about a million texts. Reading the very last text at the top of her screen, she was in disbelief that amazingly, Trent had finally made his way to her house. Making sure that her towel was secure, Shia walked over to the floor to ceiling windows in her bedroom that faced the street and almost laughed aloud at how pitiful Trent looked sitting on the step in the midst of all his belongings that she had neatly placed on the lawn before getting into her bath. Realizing that he now had a captive audience in Shia, Trent went all out jumping up and yelling at the top of his lungs.

"Shia! Baby, don't leave me out here. I was caught up. Why you acting all crazy and shit and why the hell doesn't my key work?"

Smirking as she left the window passing by the old door locks sitting on her nightstand. Shia began her nightly bed ritual. She was happy with her decision to be done with him and didn't care if the neighbors called the police on Trent outside disturbing the peace. Curling up in her bed, she allowed Trent's screams and rants to serenade her to sleep.

THE PRESENT

Chapter Twelve

Today was the fifth anniversary of the day he had taken away his own personal misery. Exiting the restaurant in the shadow of his prey, he pulled his hat down lower on his head and readjusted his sunglasses as he continued in motion behind her. Spending the last seven years studying her every move, he was now ready to settle an old vendetta. The world had to know. More importantly, they had to know.

Shia was so caught up in chasing the vendor down to get a chili dog that she never saw the mysterious man, until she ran straight into him that is. Dropping her clutch and all the papers, she'd held in her hands, she was thoroughly embarrassed. Reaching down to grab her clutter, she was even more so humiliated when she glanced up and saw how handsome the stranger was.

"Do you need help?" The stranger asked her.

"No, no," she hurriedly replied as she continued picking her things up off the ground, "This was completely my fault." The stranger extended his hand to her as she attempted to get up. Ignoring his hand, she was almost full on her feet again until a boy gliding by on his skateboard brushed by her on the sidewalk and sent her and her things in an avalanche to the ground. With an amused grin, the stranger offered his hand again.

"Now will you accept my help?"

Shia turned as red as a tomato. Seeing as to how she must have looked a heinous sight out in the middle of Manhattan, laid out on the sidewalk in the midst of her things. All she was trying to do was get a chili dog. Who knew that it would turn into a three-ring circus?

"I would love some help." She responded as she graciously grasped his outstretched hand. Making sure she was sturdy on her feet the nice stranger bent down and retrieved her things off the ground for her.

"Thank you so much. I didn't mean to make you a part of a sidewalk collision."

"It's no problem at all. I shouldn't have been in your way. I underestimated the importance of the all mighty chili dog." He said with a hint of a smile in his voice.

Laughing at his comment, Shia was glad that he had a sense of humor. Some of her embarrassment began to fade. She felt comfortable with him.

"You have no idea how serious it is. Can I treat you to one?"

"No thank you." The stranger glanced down at his watch, "I really must get going." Shia was loath to let him out of her sight.

"Well, will you allow me to take you out to dinner sometime? It's the least I can do for your kindness in helping this damsel in distress."

"I would hardly classify you as a damsel in distress. But dinner does sound nice. I think I'll take you up on your offer."

"Wonderful!" Reaching into her clutch, Shia was excited that she had a reason to pull out her new business card. She was now an art buyer for the Museum of Modern Art and loved her new job. "I'm Shia and this is my contact information," she said as she handed him the card.

Enclosing the card in his big strong hands he replied, "I'm Demetri and I will be in touch."

As suddenly as he had appeared, he disappeared the same way. Turning back to the street vendor, she was still determined to have her chili dog. She was extremely proud of herself. She asked out a guy all on her own. Smiling with satisfaction as she reached for her chili dog and paid the vendor, she had done well. Remi would be proud of her.

Demetri was elated. She made his job easy for him. When he'd intentionally stepped into her path forcing her to run into him when he noticed she wasn't paying attention, he'd never expected her to give him her business card and ask him out. Funny how things work out he thought as he watched from the shadows as Shia bought her chili dog and made her way back into the office building.

Returning home after work Shia was happy to walk into the house and see Remi sitting on the sofa eating an ice cream cone watching TV.

"Remi, you will never guess what I did today. Not even in a million years."

"Won the jackpot?" She asked without taking her eyes away from the show she was absorbed in.

"No silly. Trust me, if I'd won the jackpot I would have been calling you from an airport on my way to Tahiti somewhere, not standing here trying to get your attention."

"Sorry Shy, this may favorite show. As soon as a commercial comes on I'm all ears ok?"

Shia shook her head, "Fine. I'll change and come back."

"Cool." Remi said, taking a lick of her ice cream; refocusing on the screen.

Shia came back down the stairs ten minutes later only to find Remi engrossed in another show. Marching herself up to the television, she cut it off.

"Shy, what the hell? It was just getting to the good part."

"I want you to listen to what I have to tell you."

"Oh, yeah, I forgot you did come in wanting to talk." Leaning back into the plush sofa cushions, Remi put the last of her ice cream cone in her mouth and chewed her heart out,

"What's up?" She mumbled around her chewing.

Flopping down on the chaise next to the sofa, Shia curled her feet underneath her.

"I met a guy today and gave him my number."

Reaching for the remote, Remi seemed unenthused. "That's great Shy. I hope it works out for you." She said as she cut the TV back on.

"Umm hello," Shia said, standing to wave her hands in front of Remi before cutting the TV back off, "This is me we're talking about. I never just hand my number over to guys. Aren't you the one always telling me that I need male attention and should be more aggressive? Can I get like a pat on the back or something? I've been waiting all day to tell you about it."

Remi hopped off the sofa. "My bad Shy. You are right!" She gave her older sister a hug, "I want to hear all about it."

Shia cut her eyes at Remi. She couldn't tell if she was patronizing her or not, but she didn't really care. Either way she was going to give her an ear full.

"We met on the side walk or I should say collided. It was crazy embarrassing."

"Shy, I'm sure it was great." Remi said in a bored tone.

"Ok, ok. I can see you're not interested." Shia said rolling her eyes, "You could have at least faked a little longer for me."

Remi looked at Shia as if she were crazy.

"Now you know I am no good with that whole faking thing." Remi said cutting the T.V. back on.

"Fine." Shia replied exiting the room as she heard her cell begin to ring in the kitchen where she'd left her purse.

Remi was happy that she could return to watching her show in peace.

Picking up her cell, Shia didn't recognize the number ringing her phone.

"Shia speaking, how may I help you?"

"I called because I was hoping you would plan to collide into me again sometime soon."

Shia smiled as soon as she recognized the voice on the other end of the phone.

"Hi Demetri." Shia wanted to tell him that he could collide into her anytime.

"Hi." He paused before continuing, "Are you free tomorrow evening?"

"I may be. What do you have in mind?" She asked him.

"Dinner. Will you join me?" He asked her.

Shia smiled at the phone, "I would love too."

"Good, I'll send you the information in the morning. You have a good night."

"Thanks you too. See you tomorrow night." Shia said before hanging up the phone.

* * * *

Demetri knew it wouldn't be long before he had Shia eating out the palm of his hand. She was ripe for the picking as he liked to say. They were meeting up at Salud Restaurant in the Financial District and he was so eager it was making him nervous.

Waiting at a corner table listening to the band Demetri was anxious to see what Shia was like. He was trailing all the sisters for the last few years and Shia was the first to afford him the opportunity to meet her face to face.

"Hi," Shia said breathlessly, “Sorry I'm late." She was somewhat out of breath after rushing to the restaurant, "But the A train wasn't running, so I had to wait and catch the C to Penn Station then hop the E. It was a mess, but I'm finally here. How are you?" Shia finished her statement with a smile.

Demetri stood at her arrival and pulled out her chair, "Better now." He replied returning her smile.

"That's good to hear. This is a nice place." Shia said looking around the restaurant after taking her seat. She loved the serenity of it all. It was very quant. Not too big or too small. "Will you allow me to buy you dinner tonight, since you wouldn't allow me to buy you a chili dog?"

Demetri chuckled lowly, "No. I won't allow it. Dinner is on me."

"That's fine, but one of these days I'm going to buy your dinner and you are going to like it." Shia said in a light flirty tone.

"Ok. Sounds like a deal." Demetri was impressed with Shia's whole attitude. He enjoyed when women stepped in and offered to pay for things. It made him think of his ex-wife who was a lot like that.

"I've never been here before. What do you recommend?" Shia asked Demetri.

"The Pollo Al Horno is good."

Before Shia could answer, she saw people get out of their seats and begin to dance in tune with the music the band was playing and her eyes lit up.

"Oo, let's dance." She said smiling up into Demetri's eyes.

"I'd rather talk to you." Demetri told her.

"Oh, ok." Shia responded slightly disappointed, "My sisters would love this place."

"You have sisters?" Demetri asked her though he already knew the answer to his question.

"I have two." Shia said in merriment, "I have a twin named Leigh, and then we have our sister Remi whose seven years younger than us."

"Nice. When do I get to meet the family?"

Demetri was surprised that he was enjoying himself. Even though the evening was young, he was having a nice time with Shia. He loved the way her eyes lit up and twinkled like stars when she talked about her sisters.

Shia laughed, "Ummm, moving kinda fast don't you think? I'm not even sure if I even like you yet." She said smugly.

"You like me." Demetri gave her a lazy smile, "Or you wouldn't be sitting here having dinner with me."

Shia couldn't help herself. She broke into a smile.

"Well, you may be right." She said pushing her long hair behind her ear. She wished she had worn it in an up do instead of down.

"I am." Demetri told her.

Shia laughed and shook her head at his statement. Men and their cockiness he thought to herself as the waiter came over and she ordered the dish Demetri had recommended and enjoyed the rest of her evening.

Chapter Thirteen

Shia had a headache. Leigh and Remi were blasting Jay Z's Blueprint CD and dancing crazily around the living room. Normally, she would have joined in, but tonight all the noise was making her headache worse. She had a lot on her mind.

"I've decided to marry Demetri."

"What!" Leigh shouted over the music as she picked up the remote to turn down the music, "Sorry Shy, what did you say?" She asked looking at Shia.

"I've decided to marry Demetri."

"Why?" Remi asked as she continued dancing even though Leigh had already cut the music off.

"Are you serious?" Leigh said asking her question at the same time as Remi.

"Yes, I'm serious." Shia told Leigh, "And because I think it's the right thing to do." She said to Remi.

Leigh was taken off guard, "I don't think that's a good idea." Leigh said sitting next to Shia, "I think you're just missing Trent, so you jumping at the first guy who shows you any attention."

"Hey, that's uncalled for. Trent and I haven't been together in two years. I mean, how long do you expect me to be single?" Shia now had an attitude on top of her headache, "Just because you haven't dated since Kodi, don't you sit there and judge me."

Remi could tell by Shia's tone that she was upset, which meant that she and Leigh were about to get into it and Remi wanted no parts of it. She hated having to choose sides between her sisters, so she went to the kitchen to make herself something to eat.

"Why are you bringing up Kodi? I've been done with that whole bullshit situation, but you lying to yourself saying you're done with Trent."

"Seriously Leigh, you're working my nerves. There is nothing to say about Trent. He and I are done. So drop it! I'm just letting you know what's going on with me. I'm getting married, why can't you be happy for me?"

"Because I feel like you're making a big mistake. You've only been dating this guy for a few months. Why would you marry someone you barely know?" Leigh was truly shocked by Shia's behavior; this was so out of character for her.

"If you take out the time to get to know him a little more maybe you would feel differently."

"It's too fast, Shy. I'm not trying to judge you. I'm just saying you should think about it a little more first."

Shia bit down on her lip. She knew the marriage was sudden, but it's something she wanted to do and she wanted her sister's support.

"What if I invited him over to give you and Remi an opportunity to just get to know him better?" Shia turned questioning eyes to Leigh. "What do you think?"

"Obviously this means a lot to you." Leigh said taking a deep breath, "Sooo, you can bring him over for me and Remi to check him out...again."

Leigh knew Shia wanted her to be excited about her engagement, but she couldn't find it in herself to do it. She knew did down Shia wasn't over Trent, but for the sake of argument, she would give Demetri a do over.

Leigh remembered the first time she had met Demetri. It was by mistake when she was on a lunch break from her journalist job at The New Yorker and had decided to make a run to Cosi on 56th street for a sandwich. The exchange was far from warming. Even though Demetri could pass as a tall, dark handsome cousin of Morris Chestnut, there was something about him that crept Leigh out. When he looked at her with his piercing brown eyes, it was almost as if he were searching for her soul.

Shuddering at the memory, she wasn't looking forward to another meeting with him anytime soon, but to make her sister happy she would do what she had to do.

* * * *

"Remi can you pass me the corn please?" Shia said as she watched Remi pick up the container holding the corn and pass it to her.

It was so quiet in the dining room you could hear a pin drop. This was the night Shia had invited Demetri to dinner and both her sisters were acting like mutes.

"Ahem." Shia cleared her throat, "Leigh, Demetri likes to read mysteries like you do, why don't you ask him about some books that he's read?" Shia asked attempting to break the ice.

Leigh narrowed her eyes evilly at Shia. "The only question I want to ask and get the answer to from this guy is why he wants to marry my sister so fast?" Leigh said directing her statement at Shia. "I'm sitting right here." Demetri said staring a hole in Leigh's forehead, "You can ask me directly."

"Fine," Leigh said nastily as she turned and faced Demetri, “Why are you marrying my sister? You two barely know one another. It can't be love, so what is it?"

"I do love Shia."

"Yeah, right. You haven't known her long enough to love her." Leigh stared him straight in the eye, "And I don't trust you."

"Leigh enough!" Shia was tired of her smart mouth.

"Well, I'm happy for you two." Remi chimed in sensing Shia's frustration.

Shia gave Remi a grateful smile. "Thanks Remi." She said taking a sip of her drink.

"Girl, cause you need someone to keep the cob webs off Ms. Kitty. Seems to keep you happier." Remi laughed.

Shia's eyes widened as she accidentally spat out her drink at Remi's outrageous comment and turned beet red.

"Remi that is inappropriate for the dinner table in front of company." Shia chastised her.

"He's practically family now Shy. Lighten up." Remi replied.

"He won't be if I have anything to do with it." Leigh interjected snidely.

"You don't have anything to do with it." Demetri spoke up. Eyeing Leigh in disdain. He could tell this sister was going to be a problem and he always tried to avoid problems.

Leigh refused to cower under Demetri's intense gaze. There was something about him that just rubbed her the wrong way and she was done with the situation.

"Excuse me; I've had enough of dinner. I'm going out." Leigh said placing her fork on her plate and scooting her chair back as she stood up, "I refuse to be a part of this." Leigh said as she left the kitchen.

"I'm sorry about this." Shia apologized to Demetri and went after Leigh leaving Remi alone at the table with Demetri.

"What is wrong with you?" Shia demanded of Leigh when she caught up with her in front of the hall closet.

"No Shy, what is wrong with you should be the question." Leigh pointed out as she removed a sweater from the closet and looked at her sister closely, "Why are you doing this? I don't care what you say, you don't love this guy and you know it. I can tell. I know you. What's really the deal? What's going on with you?" Leigh asked putting the sweater on.

"Because I want a family. We're not getting any younger you know."

"Shy, there's nothing wrong with that, but why not give it some time?"

Shia was tired of having the same conversation with Leigh over and over.

"Lei Lei, why can't you just support me and my decision, like I would do for you?"

Leigh opened the front door and looked back at Shia, "Because I just can't Shy, I can't." She said before walking out and closing the door behind her.

Chapter Fourteen

Laughing as Demetri ran and jumped into the pool head first, Shia couldn't believe her good fortune. It was three years since the two of them had collided on the middle of a crowded sidewalk in Manhattan. Who could have guessed that the random stranger would become her husband and father to their beautiful one-year-old twin boys? Life couldn't be any better for her.

"Mama." Shia instantly smiled. The boys had just learned to talk and she relished in hearing them calling her Mama. Nothing in life ever compared to the sound of those magical words. They were both in the pool playing with Demetri waving at her.

She waved back as Remi and Leigh came and sat beside her. Both her sisters were still living with her and from the looks of things they did not intend to move out anytime soon.

"I love those little guys." Remi said as she sat at the bottom of Shia's lawn chair and waved at the boys.

"I said it at the wedding and I'll say it now, I do not like Demetri. I don't know what possessed you to marry him."

Shia let out a sigh, "Leigh you let it be known how you feel all the time about Demetri. Can we have a day of peace please? Goodness."

"Fine," Leigh huffed as she glared at Demetri in the distance. Something about Demetri still rubbed her the wrong way. Leigh knew he was up to no good. She could feel it all through every bone in her body.

"I'm just saying, I think after Mommy and Daddy dying and then you and Trent going back and forth that you rushed into this whole marriage thing. I mean, do you really love him?" Leigh asked Shia eyeing her intently.

Shia let out an exasperated sigh. She didn't understand why Leigh was bringing this up for the umpteenth time.

"Yes, I love my husband." Shia said slow and deliberate so Leigh would get the point and leave her alone.

"Do you really? Because I remember how you used to look at Trent and I've never seen you look at Demetri that way. Not once, even on your wedding day." Leigh snapped back snaking her neck to the side.

"Leigh, not now okay. We're trying to have a nice drama-free day. Why are you so determined to ruin it?"

Leigh rolled her eyes.

"I didn't know talking about the love of one's husband could ruin a day." She shrugged as she stood up, "Guess I was wrong. Enjoy your day without me. I'm going out."

"Good riddance." Shia shouted after her. Leigh with her unsolicited comments had completely altered Shia's mood. She didn't like having spats with her sister for one and two now thanks to Leigh, she was beginning to have doubts about Demetri. She'd never looked at it from the angle Leigh had looked at it. Maybe the issues with Trent and then their parents dying pushed her right into Demetri's waiting arms, but he'd never made her unhappy. The last couple of years were great. Maybe the chemistry she and Trent once shared wasn't there, but Demetri was a wonderful provider and father to their sons. All relationships didn't need that fiery can't get enough chemistry. That type of chemistry was dangerous anyway. She and Demetri were comfortable. He was a safe bet and sure thing, unlike Trent.

Shia looked over at Remi. "Can you believe her? Always meddling in other people's business."

"I'm staying out of it. You and Leigh do this all the time. I'm not picking sides and I don't have an opinion either way." Remi said as she got up, walked over to the pool, and jumped in to play with the boys. Shia smiled at that. Anyone could see that Remi loved being an auntie and she loved it.

* * * *

Leigh didn't care what Shia thought. She knew something was up with Demetri and she was determined to find out what it was. The first day she'd met him, she'd felt an eerie tingle go down her spine. She wasn't entirely sure at the time, but there was something familiar about him, as if maybe they had met before.

She wished the house she'd grown up in was still accessible, but after her parent's death and the house half burned down to the ground, there was nothing to return to Maryland for. That was why Shia and Remi had relocated to New York to be with her.

Retreating to the hall closet, she pulled out a box of her mother's belongings. This box is all that was left after her parent's death. It was found in her mother's car. Leigh had never bothered to go through the box because her mother really wasn't one of her favorite people, but right now she needed answers and her instincts told her Demetri was somehow related to their past life in Maryland. She couldn't put her finger on it just yet, but there was something about him that was vaguely familiar.

Pulling the lid off the box, Leigh wondered what she would find inside. Seeing folded papers at the top of the box, she unfolded them and her eyes widened when she saw that they were adoption papers. Leigh's hand was shaking when she saw Shia's name listed on the first paper and her parents' signatures at the bottom. There were two more adoption papers inside the box. One with her name and one with Remi's name listed. Leigh was in shock. All three of them were adopted. How could they not have known? So many things began to make sense about their upbringing now and so much still did not. She wondered whom their real parents where since according to the papers the adoption was a private one and did not list their actual birth parents' names.

Leigh wasn't angry or sad about the situation she just wondered how Shia and Remi would take it.

Leigh put that thought aside. She would come back to that stuff, but right now she was more concerned with the mystery of Demetri.

There had to be something. Demetri was familiar to her and she needed to know why. The box had many love letters to her mother from various men she'd had affairs with through the years of her marriage.

Leigh shook her head as she read some of the letters. Her mother truly was a piece of work. She had cheated on their Dad for as long as Leigh could remember. Her parents had the weirdest relationship. Neither really did any parenting. They were both solely absorbed in themselves.

Dismissing her parents from her mind completely, Leigh continued reading the letters in the box.

Alycia,

You are my world. I can't be without you and I won't. I love you. We'll be together forever no matter what it takes. You'll see. I love you with all that's in me.
~Maxwell

As Leigh continued through the letters, she realized Maxwell must have been one of her mother's more favorable affairs because he wrote many letters, most pleading with her to leave her husband. The last letter she found from him was the saddest and most profound.

Alycia,

This has gone on long enough. I can't live like this anymore. My decision has been made. I do love you, but I have found I will have to live without you.
~Maxwell

Besides some old photos of her mother and her various lovers and the adoption papers, there was nothing else of significance in the box. Leigh closed it up and put the box in her room. She would keep the knowledge of she and her sisters adoption a secret for now until she could find out what was going on with Demetri. Vaguely remembering Shy say something about Demetri growing up in Washington, D.C. Leigh decided it was time to take a road trip.

Early the next morning Leigh walked into the living room where Remi was lying on the sofa, with her carry on bag.

"Where you going?" Remi asked when Leigh walked into the room with luggage on her shoulder.

"Washington, D.C."

Remi arched her brow, "Why?"

"I have some business to take care of. Since you're up can you take me to the airport?"

"As long as I can take you like this, we're good."

Leigh didn't even bother to give Remi the once over. Remi was always dressed nice and crazy.

"You're good. Let's go."

"Okay. Let's roll." She said rolling off the couch.

* * * *

Leigh was proud of herself. She was really contemplating going into the investigative field after all the work she had put in to find Demetri. Who knew one person could have so many secrets? Leigh just needed something concrete to show Shia, so her sister could finally see it wasn't just a hunch she had about Demetri, but that there was some validity to what she was feeling.

Walking into Demetri's old high school, she had a feeling that she was on her way to something good. An hour after she had entered the school Leigh was leaving a happy lady. Leigh knew she'd hit the jackpot. With Demetri's old high school yearbook in tow, she was going to beat Shia over the head with it if she couldn't see to reason.

Back at the airport, Leigh was surprised when she was chosen for a random security search. Following the two men into the private room off to the side of the boarding area, Leigh became uncomfortable when the door shut and the two men turned to face her. Where was a female security attendant she wondered? She thought that it was policy to have a female official present if a woman had to be searched for any reason.

"Have I done something wrong?" She asked the two men who still had yet to speak to her.

Neither responded to her question. Roughly pushing her up on the wall, one of the men handcuffed her wrists together.

"What the hell are you doing?" I haven't done anything wrong!" She screamed.

"Shut up!" Said the man who had handcuffed her as he smacked her across her face.

Leigh was in shock. What in the world was going on? Slowly running her tongue over her aching lip, she could taste the salty remnants of blood from where he had busted her lip. She could barely do that before the second man tore off tape and placed it over her mouth. Hearing the faint sound of a door closing behind her, Leigh turned her head to face the sound.

"Well, well. If it isn't little Miss Private Detective." As soon as she heard the voice and saw the face to confirm her recognition Leigh's whole body went into shock. She must be hallucinating. It couldn't possibly him.

Picking up her bag, he opened it and pulled out the yearbook.

"And exactly what did you plan on doing with this?"

Eyes nearly bulging out of her head, Leigh watched helplessly as he took out a lighter and set the yearbook to flames. Pulling all the items out of her purse, he took her ID out of her wallet and threw everything else away.

She couldn't understand what was going on and why it was all happening to her.

"You look confused. Don't worry; it will all be over soon." Was the last thing Leigh heard before something heavy was brought down on her head and the world went black?

Chapter Fifteen

"Remi, have you heard from Leigh?"

"No."

"I'm starting to get worried about her. I've tried calling her for the last two days and she hasn't called me back, which is weird for her."

"She's probably fine. You know how Leigh gets when she's in one of her moods."

"No Remi, something is wrong. I can feel it. Leigh's my twin, remember? We can feel when something isn't right with each other?" Shia turned to look at Remi, "I mean, Leigh didn't mention where she was going or anything?"

"Yeah, I took her to the airport the other day. She said she was going to Washington, D.C. for a little while." Remi shrugged, "I figured she needed some me time or something."

Shia narrowed her eyes at Remi's nonchalance about the whole Leigh situation.

"You don't think you could have just told me that?"

"Didn't think it was important."

"Whatever Remi." Shia said with a slight attitude, "I still know that something is not right.

* * * *

Trent was lonely. It was years since Shia had put him out for the last time and as crazy as it sounded, he still missed her. Phylicia was driving him out of his mind. When she'd first told Trent that she was pregnant he was skeptical. It was almost; if he'd found it funny; a comic case of déjà vu. He'd had the baby tested as soon as she was born and this time the test came back 99.99 percent accurate that he was the father.

His baby girl was his life. She'd just turned four and he couldn't imagine how he got through life before without her.

Phylicia was another story. The two of them hadn't gotten back together because Trent didn't trust her further than he could see her. She enjoyed getting on his nerves. He was at her apartment to pick up his daughter, and he was still standing at the front door ten minutes after his arrival. Knocking one final time, Trent had turned to leave, he heard the door open; turning back, he closed his eyes in a quick prayer for God to protect him this evening.

"Hey where you going?" Phylicia asked in a sultry voice.

"Stop playing games." Trent said taking in Phylicia's appearance. She was scantily clad in a red and black lace bra with the nipples cut out and a pair of matching panties with a slit in the crotch area.

"Where is Khloe?"

"She and Avionne are at my mother's. Come in." She waved him inside.

Trent took a step back.

"Why is she at your mother's? You knew I was stopping by to pick her up today. It's my day." Trent was highly irritated.

"She'll be back later tonight and you can take her for the weekend. I wanted to spend some one on one time with her daddy first."

Trent shook his head in disbelief. He couldn't knock Phylicia's hustle. She was in the game to win him and had no intentions of stopping until she got him.

"Yo P, I just want to see my daughter." He was heated that she had sent Khloe with Avionne to her mother's.

Phylicia opened the door a little wider.

"Trent I promise my mom will bring her home in a little bit. I want you to be my entertainment for a little while," she said slowly running her fingertips over her hardened nipples. That got Trent's attention and he felt himself becoming aroused.

"P, you know we don't get down like that." Trent sighed in a halfhearted attempt to get Phylicia to lay off him.

Phylicia could feel him weakening. She couldn't understand why he made it a point to deny her every time they had sex. They had sex at least twice a week ever since Khloe was born, but Trent fought her every step of the way every time. Just once, she wanted him to act as if he wanted to do it without her practically begging for it.

"Hey…hey." Trent gently touched Phylicia's arm to capture her attention. "I'm not going to come in." He could see the water push to the surface of her eyes, but he was going to be strong and smart with this situation. "We can't get it in like we used too. I have to move on with my life. I have to." Trent watched as Phylicia lowered her head. He gently lifted her chin up with his hand, so she had to look him in his eyes.

"Part of me will always love what we had together back in the day, but I did what I was supposed to do. I loved you like women dream of being loved and now I doubt all women, which can explain why I haven't been in a real relationship since."

Trent's mind wandered back to Shia. There was something about her that he couldn't get off his mind. He'd heard she'd gotten married and he kept trying to tell himself that he was happy for her, but the truth was if Phylicia hadn't popped up pregnant, he and Shia may have had a chance at something real.

"So you're blaming me for your lack of being able to get into a relationship?"

"Yes." Trent said looking down at her. Grabbing his phone as it vibrated on his hip.

"Aye T, what it do?"

"Yo what's up? Ain't nothing going on, on my end." Trent listened on the phone as he mouthed the words, "I'll be by tomorrow to pick up Khloe. Have a good night." He said as he turned and walked down the steps out of Phylicia's building never looking back to see her reaction.

"I'm in town. What you got planned for the night? Want to hit the club?" Kodi asked.

Since he hardly got to see him anymore Trent knew it was a good opportunity to hang with Kodi. He and Sherri had moved out of state a couple of years ago so Kodi could put space between his family and Leigh after the whole kid incident. But Trent wasn't in the mood for the club.

"Nah, I think I'm a chill tonight."

"Oh aight bet. You home? I want to run something by you for a second."

"I'm headed that way now. Meet me there in ten."

"Bet." Kodi responded before hanging up the phone.

* * * *

"Baby, I'm worried about Leigh. She's been gone a week. I'm thinking about filing a missing persons report on her."

Demetri looked up from the paper he was reading giving Shia his undivided attention.

"Didn't Remi say she went out of town?"

"Well, yes…"

"Then what's the problem?"

Shia shook her head in disbelief. Why was no one worried about Leigh's whereabouts but her? "The problem," Shia stated in the slow patient tone, "Is that she hasn't returned not one of my phone calls."

"So," Demetri stated in nonchalance, "Didn't you two have some type of disagreement before she left? Maybe she doesn't want to talk to you."

"Whatever." Shia sighed in frustration at his response. She opened her mouth to say more, but was cut short due to the phone ringing.

"Hello." Shia answered after the first ring.

"Oh my God! What happened?"

Demetri jumped up when he heard Shia's frantic reaction to whatever she was hearing on the phone.

"Do you know when?" She asked, "Yes. Ok. I can be at the airport in about thirty minutes. I'll see you when I arrive. Thank you."

Shia hung up the phone in tears. Demetri pulled her into a hug.

"What's going on babe?"

"That was the Metropolitan Police Department. They found Leigh's belongings at the airport in a trash can. She is officially reported missing. I knew something was wrong. I knew it." Shia whispered burying her head into Demetri's chest.

Chapter Sixteen

Holding a picture frame that held a photo of she and Leigh when they were first about to embark on their separate college journeys, tears slowly began to slide down Shia's face. She felt as if she had entered the twilight zone. Nothing was as it should be. For the life of her, she still couldn't believe that Leigh was missing. She felt like someone had ripped her body in two. Her twin, the other half of her was gone. She could feel Leigh though, which was a great thing. It meant that she was still alive. Now it was just a matter of finding her, so she stayed that way.

Putting the photo back into her purse, Shia glanced over at Remi and smiled. Remi had her earphones in her ears and was jamming to her iPod. Oh, to be twenty-four again. Those seven years that separated them weren't many by counting standards. But by living actual life standards, it was like an eternity. Sighing as she watched the clouds coast by, she dreaded when they finally landed in Washington, D.C. The detectives there had called and asked them to come down to view the surveillance tape from the airport security cameras. Shia still couldn't understand what Leigh was doing in D.C. to begin with.

When she and Remi arrived at the terminal at National, the detectives were waiting for them.

"Ms. Cunningham?" One of the detectives asked while approaching Shia with a photo of her in his hand.

"Yes, that's me." Shia responded shaking his outstretched hand, "And this is my sister Remi." She said as she motioned towards her.

"Good, please follow us. This shouldn't take too long." He said in a southern drawl as he escorted the two of them to his squad car.

"This is so weird." Remi whispered to Shia in the backseat of the squad car.

Shia glanced at her, "Why? Do you feel like you're under arrest?"

"Something like that." Remi replied, "I don't like it at all."

"You'll be fine. Just be calm."

Remi shifted around the seat a little.

"Ummm, there's something I should tell you before we go in."

Shia sighed, "Rem, what is the matter? Since when did you start beating around the bush about stuff; which is what I feel like you are doing."

Now Remi was fidgeting with her purse handle acting as if she was anxious about something. Unfortunately, Shia didn't have time to focus on her because they had arrived at the precinct.

"Ok ladies," The detective began as he opened the back door for them, "Come this way so we can begin."

He led Shia and Remi into a back room where the lead detective on the case was waiting for them. As soon as she saw him, she gasped. The lead detective was none other than Kodi, Leigh's old sex toy or whatever you wanted to call him. What was going on she began to wonder.

"You had something to do with this, didn't you? I know you did!" Running at him the tears began falling from Shia's eyes as she attacked Kodi. Where is my sister you bastard?"

The two detectives came and restrained her as Remi stood there in confusion.

"Shia why are you attacking him. He's trying to help."

"Remi stay out of it! You don't know what you're talking about." Shia shouted.

"I know you're acting crazy." Remi stated as she watched the detective try to calm Shia down.

"Ms., you're going to have to behave yourself or you leave us no choice but to book you on assault charges."

That made Shia relax. She couldn't afford to be locked up, especially having Leigh still missing and two little ones at home.

"I will behave myself if someone tells me what he is doing here." She said pointing at Kodi.

"Detective Kodi is heading up this case."

"I'll be damned. We'll see about this. Remi let's go." Shia moved toward the door. She needed to find the real person in charge because this was nonsense.

"Shia, I want to find your sister as well. Please stay and hear me out."

Shia whirled around so fast she almost gave herself whiplash.

"You treated Leigh like trash! I didn't forget a damn thing about you!" He wanted to come in here with his overly starched uniform and badge as if he was this holier-than thou individual and Shia wasn't having it.

"Please calm down." Kodi said slowly walking over to her.

"Shia, who is he? Why are you acting this way? You never behave so badly. You are starting more and more to act like Leigh."

"Remi, I thought I told you to stay out of it."

"Shy, I'm not a little kid anymore. You can't boss me around all the time like you used to. I'm gown now. It's time you accepted that."

Shia could not believe Remi's audacity. This was not the time for a little sister breakthrough, come to Jesus moment or whatever she was having.

"Fine Remi, whatever." Turning her attention back to Kodi, "Please explain how you plan to help."

Clearing his throat, he began to sweat, speaking slowly. Remi began to wonder who was really in charge here. It seemed as if Shia was calling the shots.

"When, I found out it was Leigh that was abducted, since I knew her personally I took the case to ensure her safe return. I know things didn't go that great when she and I used to deal with each other back in the day, but things are different now. I'm different."

"Mmmhmmn. I believe that when I see it." Shia wasn't in the buying mood and she wasn't shopping around for bullshit today, "Where is this video you flew us down here to see?"

"Shia," Kodi was still trying to get her to understand.

"Kodi, enough of that." Shia had an attitude now, "Can you just show us the video please?"

"Shy, maybe we shouldn't watch it after all."

Shia couldn't believe Remi said that. This could be their one lead to getting Leigh back.

"Remi you have lost your mind. Show us the video please." She said to Kodi. Shia couldn't understand what Remi's deal was today she wasn't acting like herself. If anything was weird, it was her.

"Ok, focus on the monitor. This is the airport's surveillance and the last trace we have of your sister on file."

Shia heard Kodi speaking, but she was completely absorbed in what she was witnessing on the screen. She couldn't believe that right there in her face were Leigh's last accounted for minutes before her abduction. What shocked her the most was that she could identify three different people in the security cameras. She could see Trent talking to a stewardess. Demetri was standing next to an exit sign sipping something in a cup and constantly looking around, but the real kicker and what had her in undeniable disbelief, was right there on the surveillance footage was Remi. The detectives may not have recognized her, but Shia would know her baby sister anywhere. Shia didn't want to believe it. Standing about two feet from Demetri in a brown shoulder length wig with sunglasses and a business suit, Shia almost didn't recognize her…almost. That was the most normal she had ever seen Remi look, a far cry from the eccentric girl standing in the room with her. Slowly turning her head to look into Remi's eyes, she noticed that Remi had left the room. Shia instantly felt panic.

"Where did my sister go?"

"She stepped out as you were viewing the tape. Must have been difficult for her to watch."

I'll bet it was. Shia thought to herself.

"Do you recognize anyone besides your sister Leigh in the surveillance? Does anything stand out as suspicious to you?"

Shia honestly didn't know what to tell Kodi or the other detectives. She knew that Kodi recognized Trent, so why hadn't he mentioned anything? The whole thing seemed like a set up. Shia was mentally trying to calculate as quickly as her brain would allow. Why were Trent, Demetri, Remi and Leigh all at Metropolitan airport to begin with? And this obviously meant Trent knew Demetri, but how were all of them tied together. And how is it that Kodi, one of Trent's best friends happened to be lead detective on the case. Nothing was adding up as it should be. Shia needed time to think.

"No, I don't recognize anything suspicious." She said staring directly into Kodi's eyes, "Do you?"

"No." Kodi responded never flinching.

Right then and there, Shia went with her gut instinct. She couldn't trust anyone. She just wanted to find Leigh and now she knew that she was going to have to do it alone.

"Can you take me back to the airport please?"

"Ma'am wouldn't you like to wait for your sister to return."

Shia looked at the detective who had spoken as if he were crazy. Remi was a liar as far as Shia was concerned. She was now a suspect on her list as well.

"No, since she left she'll find her own way back. I have to go." As Shia walked out of the precinct with the two detectives who had brought her and Remi from the airport, she was surprised to see Remi standing outside by the police car as if everything was normal.

"So, this is where you disappeared to?" Shia narrowed her eyes as she continued speaking, "Why didn't you stay and watch the surveillance video with me?" She asked eyeing Remi intently waiting for her response.

Remi shrugged, "Just not interested I guess."

As Shia stared her down, Remi refused to blink. They rode in silence all the way to the airport and even on their flight; Shia had absolutely nothing to say. She didn't trust Remi now. She never knew if she would again.

Chapter Seventeen

Returning to New York, Shia was a complete mess. She had no idea what to make of the situation that had taken place in Washington, D.C. She didn't trust Remi further than she could see her. Demetri was also suspect to her now. It just didn't make sense. Why were Trent, Demetri and Remi all at the same airport at the same time where Leigh was when she disappeared and no one acted as if they knew anything?

Neither of them was speaking and that worried her, but she wondered if Trent's number were the same. Maybe just maybe he would be willing to talk to her. She needed answers and she felt like Trent would tell her something. All she needed was something to go off to give her some type of lead.

Grabbing the cordless phone in the hall as she went into the twin's nursery, shut, and locked the door behind her. She was determined to get answers. Dialing the only number she had on file for Trent, she sent up a short silent prayer to God and patiently waited as the phone rang on the other end of the receiver.

"Damn D. It took you long enough to get at me." Shia was shocked when Trent's voice came across the other end of the phone and the fact that obviously he had her and Demetri's home number in his phone and was familiar enough with Demetri to call him D.

"This isn't Demetri Trent. It's Shia." As soon as Trent heard Shia's voice, he hung up the phone. Shia's shock instantly turned to fear. What in the world was going on? Pressing the off button on the phone all Shia could think was this was not happening. It was just too much shadiness going on and not enough answers. Unlocking the door and walking out of the boy's room into the hall, she placed the phone back in its cradle. Shia had work to do; it was painfully obvious that if Leigh was going to make it back home alive in one piece, Shia was going to have to be the one to make that happen. But how, she thought."

Following the sounds of the noisy threesome, she made her way into the family room where the twins and their dad were all lying on the floor watching, "Alvin and the Chipmunks the Squeakquell."

"Baby, can we talk for a minute? The boys should be ok we won't go far."

"We can talk right here." Demetri responded without glancing her way.

"Well could you at the very least turn and look at me so I know you're paying attention?"

Demetri sighed softly, and then slowly got to his feet. Looking down on her through slit eyes she could tell he wasn't happy to be interrupted.

"What is it?" Demetri wasn't in the mood for whatever it was Shia wanted to discuss. He could tell by the serious expression on her face and the tone of her voice that any topic she had in mind was going to be draining and all he wanted to do was enjoy time with the boys.

Shia sat on the sofa in the far back of the room and motioned for him to join her.

"I'm not in the mood for some heavy confrontation with you today. I'm just trying to relax." Demetri said as he sat on the sofa next to her.

"Well sorry to interrupt your relaxation period, but I haven't been able to relax for weeks with Leigh missing. And you haven't had time to talk to me since I got back from Washington, D.C."

Demetri sighed long and hard.

"Well since you want to sit over there huffing and puffing, how about you explain to me what you were doing in the surveillance video when Leigh disappeared. You, Trent and Remi? Let's see you huff and puff your ass out of this one."

Shia was fed up with all of it. No one seemed to notice or care that Leigh was missing and she wasn't having it. Leigh was her flesh and blood, never mind her identical twin. She had to find her no matter what it took.

"Boys go to the play room and get your ninja toys and bring them back so we can play." Demetri called out to the boys. Once they left the room, he focused his attention on Shia.

Standing up and grabbing her by the throat in one fluid motion. Demetri flexed his fingers as he watched Shia struggle to breathe while her legs dangled in the air. Pulling her face close to his, he began to whisper in her ear.

"I don't have to explain shit to you. Now listen carefully you and your sisters don't mean shit to me."

Shia was frantically clinching his fingers trying to loosen his grip from around her neck so she could breathe. All while her brain also tried to zone in on the words coming out of his mouth.

"All I care about are my boys and if it comes between me and them, they can go too."

Flexing his fingers again around her throat Demetri stared into her panic-stricken eyes.

"It's in your best interest to let this thing with your sister slide. No one gives a shit but you. You ever stop and think about that?" Without waiting for Shia to respond he continued, "Any mention of this conversation to anyone and the boys will end up missing next, or buried in the backyard." He shrugged, "Your choice." Letting her neck go abruptly, Shia fell back onto the sofa as the boys reentered the family room with their ninja toys in tow. Watching as Demetri ushered them in toward the T.V. with their toys and played with them on the floor, while Shia tried to suck the air back into her oxygen-deprived lungs.

* * * *

Trent felt like a fool. He never should have hung up on Shia but he hadn't expected her to call him. He wished he'd never been caught up in any of the mess that was going on. He wanted to talk to Shia, needed to talk to her, but there were so many reasons why he couldn't. His whole purpose in life was to keep his baby girl safe and sound. He wouldn't be a good dad if he did anything but that. Knowledge wasn't always a good thing. Trent had too much, but not exactly enough and wasn't sure what to do with what he did know.

Life was crazy how it worked out. He thought as he looked in on Khloe sleeping in her room. He couldn't put into words how much he loved this little girl of his. She was everything to him and he be damned if he put her into any kind of danger.

A knock on Trent's door indicated that Phylicia had arrived.

"What's up?" Trent asked as he opened the door for her.

"Hey. Khloe ready?" Phylicia asked as she and Avionne stepped inside Trent's place.

"She's napping right now." He told Phylicia as he shut the door behind them.

"I need to speak with you for a minute. Avionne go wake up Khloe and help her pack up her stuff so we can go."

"Ok Mommy." Avionne responded before skipping down the hall.

"What do you need to talk about?" Trent asked Phylicia.

"I need to go out of town on business for a while. Is it possible for you to keep Khloe and Avionne while I'm gone?"

Trent looked at Phylicia as if she were crazy. Khloe was his daughter so that was fine, but Avionne was Phylicia's ex-husband daughter and that was a whole other story.

"Why can't Avionne stay with her father?" He inquired.

"Because he'll be out of town as well and I would like for the sisters to be able to stay together. Please Trent; it's only for a week." Phylicia raised pleading eyes up to meet Trent's cool brown ones.

He shook his head in disbelief at Phylicia's audacity, but since it would give Khloe a play buddy, he didn't think that it would do too much harm.

"It's cool. I'll hire a nanny for the week to help me out."

"Fabulous. I really appreciate this." She said kissing him on the cheek.

"Come on girls, let's go!" Phylicia yelled down the hall.

"Mommy, something's wrong with Khloe. I tried to wake her up, but she won't wake up." Trent's heart skipped a beat as he took off running down the hall with Phylicia right on his heels. Racing into Khloe's room, Trent found his baby girl lying in her bed gasping for air, turning blue.

"Call 911!" Trent yelled to Phylicia as he immediately began CPR on Khloe. By the time the medics showed up Trent was visibly perspiring in his efforts to get his little girl breathing again. Moving aside as the professionals took over. Trent watched helplessly as they put an oxygen mask over Khloe's nose, transferred her to the gurney, and whisked her off to the ambulance.

Trent was doing his best to stay calm as he allowed Phylicia to ride in the ambulance with Khloe, while he and Avionne followed in his jet-black Audi A8.

They were at the hospital roughly twenty minutes before the doctor came back to inform them that his little Khloe was pronounced dead.

Trent felt himself wanting to go into shock, but he had to hold it together for Phylicia, who was so hysterical that hospital staff had intervened by giving her a tranquilizer to calm her down. She was now resting peacefully in one of the hospital rooms.

"I'm hungry." Trent looked down to see Avionne's wide brown eyes staring up at him. He'd honestly forgotten she was there with them.

"Why don't we call your dad, while we get you some food?" Trent pulled out his cell phone. "What's your dad's number?" Avionne rattled off the number for him. "What's your daddy's name?" he asked her.

"Maxwell."

Avionne's dad didn't answer, so Trent left a message where they were and for him to come and pick her up if he could. Then he took her down to the hospital cafeteria to eat.

Trent was grief stricken. His little princess was gone and with Phylicia completely out of it. He couldn't break down like he wanted to because someone had to be strong for Avionne, who had no idea that she had just seen her little sister for the last time. Trent was going to let Phylicia explain the situation to her because he didn't feel like it was his place to do so. However, he was anxious for her father to arrive. The hospital needed him to fill out paperwork as soon as possible.

"Hey you call me?"

"Daddy!" Avionne screamed.

Trent smarted as he recognized the sound of the voice. Taking in the speaker slowly, he was stunned.

"Not that I know of." He said rising out of the cafeteria chair. "I called a Maxwell to come and pick up Avionne.

"You're looking at him. Thanks for watching Avionne. I'll holla at you later when I don't have her."

Just as quickly as Maxwell had come, he was gone leaving Trent alone in the cafeteria to collect his thoughts.

Chapter Eighteen

Remi knew she was on thin ice with Shia, but didn't know what to do about it. Everything about her life was wrong at the moment.

"You ready?" Remi heard him ask her and wanted to cry. He was slowly breaking her down. She hardly recognized herself anymore. She wanted to scream, "NO." She wasn't ready, but knew the repercussions for that would be something she would regret even more.

Slowly standing up refusing him the satisfaction of answering his question, Remi began to follow him out of the room.

"Auntie!" The twins squealed in unison. Remi's face instantly broke into a smile as she bent down to embrace them as they both ran up to her wrapping their little arms around her legs.

God was favoring her at this very minute. He'd had Shia and the boys come home early to prevent the torture she was about to have to endure with Demetri.

"Hey munchkins. You miss me?"

"Yes." They said in unison again.

Remi's smile got even bigger.

"Come on you two; let's go watch cartoons in your playroom." She said as she rushed them down the hall.

"What are you doing back so early?" Demetri asked as soon as Shia came into view.

"Didn't know I needed a reason for coming home." Shia replied giving Demetri much attitude. She wasn't feeling him and wanted him to stay away from her and out of her space.

"Shia, let's talk about the other day."

Shia looked Demetri up and down as if he were stupid, which he must, in fact, be thinking they had anything to talk about. Since their standoff, she had moved into the guest room and was looking for a place to live. Demetri ceased to exist to her. She was done with the marriage, him, everything. She just wanted to be a good mother to her children.

"Nothing to talk about." She said before going into her room and locking the door behind her.

Pulling her laptop out, she opened her email. This was a rough couple of weeks for her. With Leigh still missing and all the shady people around her, she didn't know whom to trust. The police department in Metropolitan said they were doing everything in their power to find her sister, but she seriously doubted that with Kodi being the lead agent on the case. Shia shook her head at the craziness that was going on in her life and everyone around her.

About to close out her email Shia was surprised when an instant message popped up on her screen.

"Need to speak with you ASAP." It read from screen name BadGuy01. "Can't talk over computer or phone. Meet me at the spot."

Shia typed in ok. She was intrigued. She wanted to hear what he had to say. Shutting down her computer, she grabbed her purse; just to be on the safe side she made sure she had her razor blade and mace before running out the house. Shia saw him when she arrived at the spot. Part of her wanted to smile. Another part wanted to cry.

"Hi." She spoke softly when she was within hearing distance of him.

"Hey." He said turning to embrace her, "Long time."

"Yes, very." She replied nodding her head in affirmation. Needing the hug he gave, but not trusting him at the same time.

"You want to walk the path?"

"Sure, we can do that."

They walked in silence for a while taking in each other's presence.

"I want to apologize." The words were spoken so low Shia barely heard.

"Trent…"

"No really Shy," He said cutting her off. "I want to apologize for everything."

Shia stopped walking and he followed suit. Now that she was really looking at him, she noticed how distressed he looked.

"You ready to talk?" She asked.

"Yeah, we need to do that. Want to sit on those benches over there?"

"Ok." Shia said following him to the bench and having a seat.

"I didn't mean to hang up on you the way I did that day you called. It's just you caught me off guard and I wasn't prepared."

"Oh and you're prepared now is that it?"

"Somewhat. My daughter died a couple of weeks ago, so I don't much care about anything right now."

Shia gasped at the news of his daughter dying.

"Oh my God. Trent. I'm so sorry."

His eyes filled with tears.

"Yeah, I don't like talking about it too much. It's been a rough couple of weeks."

Shia pulled him into a hug that he instantly returned. The two of them were silent for a moment, naturally comfortable in each other's presence.

Trent pulled away first seemingly put back together for the time being.

"Why were you in the tape of my sister's disappearance?" Shia finally asked unable to keep the question back any longer.

"To keep my daughter alive." Trent suddenly began laughing hysterically, "That seems almost sordidly funny now that she's gone anyway. Everything was in vain." Trent looked over at Shia then.

"I wish I could help you more, but I can't. I was told to be at the airport that day at that time otherwise my daughter's life would be in danger and that was all.

"Who told you to be at the airport?" Shia asked Trent curious at who would want to hurt Leigh. It's true she had done some unimaginable things when they were younger, but that was years ago. For the last couple of years, she'd just been a party girl living her life however she wanted.

"I don't know who sent the request." Trent said answering her question, "I only received this in the mail," he pulled out an envelope, "With no return address."

Shia took the envelope to examine it, but nothing about it appeared abnormal.

"But you were on the video with my husband Demetri, Remi and Leigh." Shia eyed Trent intently, "Why?"

Trent was the one surprised by her statement now, "Remi was there?"

"Trent please tell me what happened. Where is Leigh?"

"Honestly Shy, I don't know."

"My job was to fly into the airport, stand at the security check point for an hour and then fly back home. I know nothing about nothing."

Shia wasn't sure if he was telling the truth or not, but her gut was saying he wasn't lying.

"How do you know my husband?" Trent felt like this was a trick question. He had only found out not too long ago that he, in fact, was tied to Demetri in many ways.

"I've known D since we were kids. He, Kodi and I used to play in little league together, but we lost contact for years. We only reconnected recently. He sought me out and so here we are."

"Wow. I had no idea that all of you knew one another."

"Yeah. Crazy how life works out."

"I know. Crazy sums it up just right."

Shia laid her head on Trent's shoulder, "I just don't know. I have to find my sister. I'm so worried about her."

"I know you are." Trent kissed Shia's forehead, as they sat in silence enjoying the comfort of each other's presence.

* * * *

Moving Day! Shia thought to herself. She was so excited she didn't know what to do with herself. She had taken off work to get the packers and movers in and out before Demetri got home from work. Reconnecting with Trent was good for her. Once he knew that she was looking for places to move he had graciously told her that there were vacancies in his building on the Upper West Side of Manhattan. She had filed for legal separation from Demetri and was exiting stage left immediately. Shia may be many things, but an abused woman was not one of them. Demetri put his hands on the wrong one. The boys, she and Remi; even though she didn't trust her, were on their way out.

Demteri was irritated with himself for leaving his briefcase at home. He worked in a law office in Brooklyn and hated to have to come all the way back to Manhattan, but he needed the documents for a pending case he had. When he arrived at his building, he saw moving trucks outside and wondered who was leaving the building. New York real estate moved quickly, so he knew he'd have new neighbors sooner than later. Curious when he reached his unit and found the door sitting open, Demetri was surprised to see most of the place empty with only a few boxes left inside.

Shia stopped short when she rounded the corner of the living room with the last box from the hall closet in her hands and saw Demetri standing there.

"What the hell are you doing?" He screamed at her.

Shia forced her feet back into motion. "Moving." She said trying to side step him. Demetri caught her arm forcing her to drop the box and slapped her into the opposite wall.

"You're not going any fucking where." Shia slowly moved her head to the side to as she tried to regain her composure while on the floor.

"Aye," one of the movers put down the box he was holding, "What's your problem? This is a lady. Don't you put your hands on her?" He turned back to Shia, "You ok ma'am?" He asked as he helped her up.

"Yes." Shia said grateful for the moving guys help. Standing in between she and Demetri the moving man waited for her to pick up her box and then escorted her out of the building.

"This ain't over you ungrateful bitch!" Demetri yelled after them.

* * * *

Shia tried to cover up the bruise Demetri had left on her face with make-up. She didn't want the boys or Remi to see her looking this way. The movers did a great job of making the new apartment livable.

The last box left to be unpacked was the one that was in the hall closet that she had picked up right before Demetri had come home unexpectedly. After making sure the boys were soundly tucked in for the evening, Shia brought the box into the bedroom and sat on the bed. Shia cut the T.V. on her favorite show Bad Girls Club, so she could have some background noise as she explored the contents of the box.

Reading her mother's old love letters, Shia could only shake her head in disappointment. She knew her mom had cheated on her dad, but she had no idea that there were so many men whom she was involved with. Even in death that lady didn't cease to amaze her.

Reaching toward the papers at the bottom of the box, Shia pulled out some official-looking documents curious to see what information they withheld. As Shia opened the first document, her demeanor went from calm to one of sheer disbelief. In her hands, she was holding what appeared to be adoption papers for her sisters and herself. Tossing the papers on the bed in shock Shia couldn't believe what she'd read.

There was a boatload of questions that she wanted to ask, to understand whose children they were and why their parents had never told them. Only one thing made sense with this newfound information; it explained why not one of them could bond with their mother and vice versa. Shia had always felt as if there was something holding their mother back from loving them like a mother should and now she knew why.

"What's all this stuff?"

So engrossed in her thoughts Shia didn't notice when Remi entered her room.

Shia looked at her baby sister for a few second before speaking. She still didn't trust her.

"Our adoption papers."

"Um huh?" Remi snatched the papers up off the bed, "Are you serious?"

"Yeah." Shia paused before continuing.

"Remi can I ask you something?"

Remi groaned inwardly. She knew at some point Shia would want to talk to her, but she really wasn't up to it tonight.

"Ok." Remi said setting on the edge of Shia's bed.

"I know we haven't talked recently because I really wasn't in a good head space with you a was hoping that you would come and talk to me, but since that doesn't seem like it is going to happen, I'll initiate the talk." Remi looked down at her hands pretending to be occupied with her fingernails.

"Why were you in the surveillance video when Leigh went missing? You were there," Shia began counting on her fingers, "Trent was there, and so was Demetri. Please tell me what happened that day. I promise not to be mad; I just want to find our sister. Leigh is our flesh and blood. Why would you be involved in something that may potentially harm her?"

"Demetri is an asshole."

Shia was taken back. Remi had always seemed to get along with Demetri unlike Leigh.

"What does that have to do with anything?"

"A lot. Mad you even married that chump. But I am so so thankful you had us all move away. You made the world better already."

Shia noticed the tears that began to gleam in Remi's eyes.

"Why are you crying?" She asked her.

Remi usually wasn't the crying type which meant that something was very wrong.

"Because I'm just so happy we no longer live with him. He made my life hell."

"Remi, where is Leigh?" It's not that Shia was being insensitive; it's just that whatever Remi's issue was with Demetri wasn't going to do anything to help Leigh, which was primarily Shia's focus at the moment.

"I'm not sure."

"That's not a good enough answer Remi. Where is she? What happened that day? I remember Leigh leaving and you coming home late. That's all I know about that day. But somebody knows something damn it and none of you are talking. This has gone on long enough. Stop the little girl shit. Where is she? Shia screamed getting in Remi's face.

"I don't know." Remi whispered back, "Honestly Shy, I don't know. Leigh asked me to take her to the airport, so I drove her. When I was on my way back an email came through on my phone from an unknown sender to dress in business attire, fly to National Airport and then leave around six p.m. That was it. The email said if I didn't comply with its wishes, then something would happen to you and the boys. That's all I know I swear. That's why I was on the video. I wasn't even aware that Trent and Demetri were there until you told me. I never saw them."

Shia couldn't believe what she was hearing and what was going on. Remi's explanation of the events surrounding Leigh's disappearance was parallel to Trent's. Someone they obviously knew had taken Leigh, but whom.

Chapter Nineteen

As much as Shia wanted to focus on her and her sisters being adopted, she couldn't. Leigh was her main priority and that's all there was to it. She was on a flight back to Washington D.C. with Trent in tow.

She'd filled Trent in on everything she knew but part of her still wondered why Kodi hadn't mentioned Leigh's case to Trent since he was heading the case. Something about Kodi heading the case didn't sit well with her.

"Trent, have you spoken to Kodi recently?"

"Not since the last time he was in New York and that was a few weeks ago." Trent answered with his eyes closed anxious to be off the plane because he couldn't get any rest.

"Oh." Shia replied, "Was that before or after Leigh's disappearance?"

"Before." Trent opened one of his eyes in time to observe Shia's look of defeat.

"He came over his last night in New York and we caught up on things like his son and Sherri." Shia perked up at the mention of Sherri's name.

"He and Sherri are still together?" That was interesting news to Shia. The wheels in her head began turning. She got to wondering if Kodi and Sherri were the reason for Leigh's disappearance. They both lived in Washington, D.C. where Leigh had gone missing and it was extremely convenient that Kodi was the head chief over the whole thing.

She wished her twin would help her out, usually they could sense one another, but this time that wasn't the case. Shia knew someone had her hidden away somewhere. She had to believe that, because the alternative was unbearable at the moment.

Seeing that Shia was deep in thought Trent want back to relaxing. Even though the reason for them coming to Washington, D.C. wasn't a good one, Trent was still happy to get away from home. Khloe's death was taking a toll on him. Everywhere he turned in his apartment. There were memories of her. It was a couple of weeks and her room still looked the same as the last day she was there. Trent knew he needed to pack all her things up, but that would make everything to real and he wasn't ready to let his baby go just yet. He still couldn't believe that she was gone.

Phylicia, on the other hand, seemed to be readjusting to her life just fine. She wanted to console Trent, but he wasn't feeling her. He knew she was probably grieving in her own way and he had to be left alone to grieve in his.

* * * *

Glad to be off the plane, Shia had booked them rooms near the airport to make it convenient for them since they had flown in so late and would be up in the wee hours of the morning winging it from day light to sun down until Shia found some type of clue to Leigh's whereabouts.

Shia had booked them separate rooms and considering that Trent was exhausted on the plane Shia didn't expect to hear from him for the rest of the night. So she was mildly surprised when a tap came at her door.

Getting up to undo the door latch, she cracked open the door to see Trent standing there with a bottle of wine.

"What in the world?" Shia was truly flabbergasted, "You do know this isn't a vacation right? We're here looking for my sister."

"Can I come in?"

"Oh, yeah sorry." Shia opened the door wider so he could enter.

Shutting the door firmly behind him Shia gave Trent her undivided attention.

"I came over with wine to help you take your mind off things for a little while, mine included. I've been so frazzled by Khloe's death that I need to have at least one night where I can forget reality, even if only for a little while."

"I can understand that." Shia said sitting Indian style on the bed, "It would be nice to forget things for a little while." Trent cut the radio on and dimmed the lights.

"Ahh, you're not trying to seduce me are you?"

"Shh," Trent softly chastised her as he uncorked a bottle of Moscato d'Asti and poured two glasses, "I'm trying to chill. Get your mind out the gutter." He said cracking a smile as he winked at her.

"Take off your clothes."

Shia jumped up off the bed. "Why?" in her mind, she could hear Leigh saying, "Don't be such a prude." The memory forced a smile out of her.

"I'm going to give you a much-needed massage." Trent said handing her a glass of wine. "Now, will you take off your clothes? I mean, it's not like I haven't seen it before." He smirked.

"That was years ago and remember, seeing ain't sampling."

"That's one of my biggest regrets." Trent said taking a sip from his wine glass.

"What are you talking about? You've tasted me before."

"True." He agreed, but I've never felt the inside of you before. That's my biggest regret, but I respect you for holding firm to your word."

"Thanks, I think." Shia said looking into her glass instead of at Trent. He obviously still carried a torch for her, marriage, babies, and all. She would be lying if she said she hadn't always wondered what it would be like to have Trent make love to her. Though they used to live together, Shia had still never given him any, as hard as it was at times, she always held true to no sex before marriage and that's what she had done. Demetri was the only man she'd ever slept with.

"I guess a massage would be okay. It would be very nice actually."

Trent removed the wine glass from her hand and placed it on the table. Grabbing both of her hands he sat on the edge of the bed and brought her body up against his. Resting his head on her stomach, he pulled her as close as he could.

"Help me forget Shy. Just for tonight I want to forget that Khloe won't be home waiting for me when I get there. Help me forget I won't see her smile and say Daddy anymore. Please help me forget," Shia felt his grip tighten around her waist, "The pain is killing me."

Shia couldn't help the tears that slid down her face as he spoke. His voice was filled with so much sadness and hurt.

"Ok." Shia whispered. She wanted to do whatever she could to ease his pain.

Stepping back to free herself from Trent's embrace, Shia untied the silk robe she had on and let it fall to the ground. She had just gotten out of the shower before Trent showed up outside her door and knew that she looked and smelled good.

Trent took in Shia's frame as he absorbed all of her, slowly letting his eyes roam up her body until his gaze met hers.

Shia felt as if time was standing still. Trent was the one for her. She understood that now. He stood and lifted her body against the full length of him before gently lying her on the king-sized bed; she couldn't understand why the two of them couldn't get it together whenever they were dating.

"Where are you, baby?"

Shia blinked twice, blushing as she realized she hadn't heard anything Trent was saying to her.

"I'm sorry. I didn't hear you."

"I could tell." Trent said with a slight smile in his voice, "You seemed a million miles away."

Continuing to stare into Trent's eyes, Shia was suddenly anxious. She had to have all of him and she needed him now, right now, at this very moment.

"I love you." Shia was shocked by her own words. She couldn't believe she's let the intensity of the moment allow those words to slip out of her mouth.

Trent was completely caught off guard by Shia's statement.

"I love you too." He said as he lowered his head to kiss her flat belly. He was struggling with his own internal war, wanting to shake himself for having been blinded by Phylicia's manipulative ways and leaving behind the woman. He knew in his heart that he had always needed.

Shia relaxed her mind when Trent had followed back with his own admission of love and allowed her body to feel and absorb what he made her feel. She felt as if her whole body was on fire. Demetri had never made her pulse race this way.

Trent worked his way down Shia's body until he found the sensitive intimate flower he was seeking. Her unique aroma excited him. He kissed on her until her moans were the only sounds heard during the night.

Chapter Twenty

"May I have directions to this high school please?" Shia asked the hotel concierge.

"Sure ma'am. I'll get that for you right away."

"Thank you." Shia replied to the nice man as she patiently waited for the address, still smiling and mind reeling from her late-night rendezvous with Trent. It was magical.

"Here you are ma'am."

"Thank you. Have a great day!" Shia told him as she joined Trent outside the hotel in their rented black Ford Focus. They'd rented a simple car so they wouldn't cause attention to themselves and raise suspicions as they investigated Leigh's whereabouts.

"You sure this is the place?" Trent asked as they pulled into the parking lot at an old run down school. Shia was shocked herself. She found it hard to believe that the school was open and functioning.

"Yeah, this is it. Very unwelcoming right?"

Trent took in his surroundings in disgust, "Very."
Entering the building, they followed the signs leading them to the main office.

"You made it." A voice said when they walked through the door.

Shia immediately smiled at the petite elderly Italian lady who had spoken.

"You must be Carol." She said holding out of her hand.

Carol pulled her into a hug, disregarding her hand, "The one and only. Come on honey, you can give me a hug. You and your sister are so identical. I knew who you were right away." She turned toward Trent, "And who is this handsome fellow with you? Your husband I presume?"

Trent smiled liking Carol instantly. He appreciated her way of thinking."

"Not yet, but hopefully someday."

Shia turned beat red as flash backs of the previous night danced across her mind.

"Such a shame what happened to your sister sweetie." Carol's voice suddenly a somber one. "She was so nice when she came here."

"Can you tell me anything about that day? Do you know why she came here?" Shia asked curiously.

"Not exactly," Carol said moving toward her desk. "She was very interested in a photo she saw in this old yearbook, but I've no clue which one."

Shia took the yearbook Carol handed to her.

"You can go into that back office and look it over if you like. If you have any questions, I'll be at my desk."

"Thank you so much, I'll come find you if I need you."

Shia and Trent entered the back office that Carol had indicated and sat next to each other at the lone table in the room, so they could view the yearbook together.

"I wonder what Leigh found." Shia said as she flipped the pages past school information, sports, and activity photo, until she came upon the student pictures.

"Oh my goodness! Is that who I think it is?" Shia exclaimed pointing at one of the pictures.

Trent glanced at the photo, but wasn't as shocked as Shia, only mildly surprised by the fact the man in the photo had gone to school down here.

"Maxwell Fulton." Shia read below the man's picture. She turned quickly to face Trent.

"Did you know about this?"

Trent shook his head, "I had no idea he want to school out here."

"I can't believe this. Everything about my life has been a lie." Tears escaped Shia's eyes. Trent pulled her into a hug attempting to comfort her.

Pulling away from Trent as she got herself together, Shia put her brain in motion.

"So, if this is all Leigh found out, why would she be taken? It doesn't make sense." Shia said pondering on her thoughts.

"Ok, it's time to leave!" Kodi yelled bursting through the door. A look of disbelief and shock overtook Kodi's face when he recognized Trent in the room with Shia.

"T, what you doing here?" Kodi asked, eyeing him suspiciously.

"What's up?" Trent dapped up Kodi, "Here with Shy researching some things."

While they continued to talk, Shia grabbed the yearbook and snuck it in her shoulder bag.

"What things?"

"I'm retracing Leigh's steps from the day she disappeared if you must know, since I can't trust the good ole Metropolitan Police Force finest to get it done." Shia interjected on their conversation staring Kodi up and down in disgust.

"We are doing everything we can." Kodi said with an edge to his voice.

"Well, I can't tell from where I'm standing. You would think you would have some type of caring or sense of obligation to her."

"Hey check this, "Kodi said trying to step in Shia's face, but Trent stood in front of her like a shield preventing that, "I don't owe your sister shit! She tried to fuck up my life. I'm doing my job to find her, but I'm not going above and beyond for her ass, by no means." He spat at her.

"You bastard!" Shia yelled as she pushed Trent's back as an attempt to get him out of her way, so she could gauge Kodi's eyes out.

"Babe, calm down." Trent said as he turned to face Shia trying to defuse the situation.

"Don't tell me you back together. T, are you crazy?" Kodi shouted.

"Excuse me, but you'll have to keep it down officer. This is a school building and morning classes are in session." Carol stated coming to the door with a stern look of disapproval, "Inside voices please."

"My apologies ma'am." Kodi responded politely as Carol backed out the office closing the door behind her.

Trent offered no explanation to Kodi about him and Shia being together. Frankly, he felt that it was none of Kodi's business.

"How did you even know we were here?" Trent asked.

"I know everything happening in my city."

Shia wanted to throw up. Kodi was such a pompous asshole. For the life of her she couldn't understand the old crush Leigh had on him. Shia just thought the whole thing was gross.

"Let's go." Shia pulled Trent by the arm as she brushed past Kodi and his ridiculousness.

"Thank you Ms. Carol. You were a tremendous help." Shia said stopping by her desk on their way out.

"Oh, you're welcome honey. Come back anytime and please let me know how things turn out with that sister of yours."

"Will do. Take care."

* * * *

Kodi knew it was only a matter of time before things hit the fan.

"What's the matter Papi?" Sherri asked coming up behind Kodi and placing her hands on his shoulders.

"Got a lot on my mind.'

"I can tell. You're so tense."

"Don't do that!" Kodi shouted as he got out the chair and retreated to his room shutting the door behind him leaving Sherri standing there confused. He was like an electric fuse recently, always ready to ignite. Hearing a shot not too long after he shut the door Sherri grew anxious. Kodi never kept bullets in his gun while he was in the house because he didn't want William to accidentally get hold of his gun and misfire it. Which meant that something was terribly wrong? Sherri ran to the bathroom door and began banging on it hysterically.

"Baby! Answer me, what are you doing in there," Sherri yelled through the door, hearing no response, she tested the knob and it was unlocked so she entered.

Kodi hadn't replied because he couldn't. Lying on the bed with a single gunshot wound to his temple, his body was hunched over in the middle of the bed.

Sherri's piercing scream could be heard all throughout the quiet neighborhood they resided in and she knew that her life would never be the same.

Chapter Twenty-One

"Remi!" Shia yelled as she entered her silent apartment after returning from D.C. Not hearing anything, she figured that Remi had taken the boys out for a little while. Putting her bags down, she ruffled through her purse for her cell phone. Her phone hadn't worked the whole time she was out of town so she'd cut it off, as soon as she cut it back on her voicemail indicated twenty messages waiting. She shook her head and wondered who called her that many times, figuring it was probably Demetri trying to threaten her into allowing him to see the boys; she ignored them, for the moment, and dialed Remi's number. When the phone went straight to voicemail, she left a message. "Hey sis, I'm back home. Call me when you get a second, so I can talk to my babies. I miss them."

Retrieving her bags from where she'd dropped them in the hallway, she was headed to her room to dissect the yearbook she had taken more in depth when she noticed the hallway closet door ajar. Shia was startled to see all the closets contents scattered on the floor. Shaking her head, she continued on to her room. Remi must not have been paying attention to the boys and as a result; her hall closet was now looking a mess. She would clean it up after she was settled.

Walking into her room Shia stopped short. Her bedroom was completely ransacked. Her mattress was flipped and on the floor, the lamps were turned over, clothes strewn all over the room, everything in her closets and drawers was emptied. Dropping her bags on the floor Shia began to panic. Quiet apartment, everything in disarray, Remi's phone going straight to voicemail, something was wrong.

Shia hated to do it, but she grabbed her cell to dial Demetri.

"You have some nerve calling me."

Shia rolled her eyes momentarily forgetting her panic, how could she have married and produced children with such an asshole.

"Did you pick up the boys while I was gone?"

"You mean when you went on your weekend vacation with you ex and abandoned your children? I have the boys now; you no longer need to worry about them."

"I would never abandon my children! If anyone is unfit it's you."Shia was livid. "I'm on my way to get them and where is Remi?"

"I couldn't care less about your sister and you won't be picking up the boys. I have been granted temporary custody pending a court hearing about their mother abandoning them."

Shia had to take deep breaths as she listened to what Demetri was telling her. She was having a what the fuck moment. Demetri had temporary custody of the boys due to her abandoning them. What the hell?

"You're so full of shit! Remi would NEVER just hand the boys over to you and say I abandoned them. WHERE IS SHE?"

"I told you I don't know where your sister is, but I do know that I am done with this conversation." Demetri hung up.

Shia was literally floored. He was not going to get away with this. She wasn't having it. Grabbing her keys, Shia left her apartment to hail a cab and head down to the police station.

"How may we help you?" The clerk at the station asked as soon as the lady entered the door. She could tell by her aggressive manner that there was a problem.

"My husband and I are separated and somehow when I went out of town over the weekend he received temporary custody of our twins while they were in the care of my sister Remi. I need someone to find out what happened right now."

"I can look into that ma'am. May I have yours and your husband's name?"

"Shia and Demetri Cunningham."

"Ok, it should only take a minute to look into this. Would you like to have a seat?"

"No I would not. I would like to know how my husband received custody of my boys." Shia was irritated and the clerk wasn't helping.

"There is an order granting him temporary custody stating that the children were abandoned. A family member by the name of Remi called into the station to say they were abandoned and she could not care for them. Phone calls to the mother; meaning you, Ma'am," The clerk said giving Shia a pointed look, "Went unanswered and there was an emergency hearing initiated by the father, a Demetri Cunningham, for temporary custody to which he has been granted."

Shia didn't believe Remi would do this to her, but the evidence was there and it was real. Tears glistened in her eyes, but she refused to cry.

"I would never abandon my boys." She whispered to the clerk.

"Be that as it may ma'am, the children were left with no one to care for them. You have a court date in a month to plead your case to the judge."

"Thank you." Shia said as she exited the station to hail a cab back home.

Returning to her building Shia headed to Trent's apartment instead of her own. Trent answered the door after one ring of the doorbell to see Shia standing there and immediately knew something was wrong by her blood shot red eyes.

"What's wrong?" He asked as Shia stepped past him to enter the apartment.

"Demetri took my boys and I'm not sure if I'll be able to get them back.

Trent enveloped her into a hug. The gently guided her toward the couch. He braced himself for Shia's reaction.

"Remi is missing."

"What?" Shia whispered shaking her head as if in a daze.

"I knew something was wrong, that girl never cuts her phone off. How do you know?"

"I received this when I got back." Trent handed Shia a letter and her heart began to sink before she read the words.

"Sad I had to do this, but you two left me no choice. Remi had to join her sister and let Shia know if she doesn't watch her step, she'll be next."

Shia dropped the letter. "What is this and why did you receive it?" She asked Trent suspiciously.

Trent shrugged, "I don't know. It was taped to my door when I got home."

"This can't be happening. First Leigh went missing. My boys have been taken from me and now Remi is missing. No." She said shaking her head, tears freely flowing, "No."

Chapter Twenty-Two

Trent ignored his phone as it began to vibrate at his hip. Right now, his main concern was Shia. She was going through a lot right now and he was doing everything within his power to console her. This time feeling his phone begin to vibrate again, Trent removed it from his hip to see who was blowing him up like this.

"P, this really isn't a good time." He said answering the phone when he saw Phylicia's name flashing across the screen.

"Kodi shot himself." He heard her whisper into the phone.

Shia felt Trent's body go rigid beneath her head and she looked up at him curiously.

"What…?" he whispered back. Trent refused to believe that he had heard Phylicia correctly.

"He's gone baby. I flew done here as soon as Sherri called me. She is an absolute wreck. I never meant for any of this to happen." She cried on the other end of the phone.

"Hey, it's not your fault." Trent heard himself say trying to sooth her and deal with his own range of emotions.

"Did Sherri say why?" He asked her as he heard a beep on his phone indicating that another call was coming through.

"Aye P, this Sherri. I'm a hit you back," He told her before clicking over not knowing if she hung up or not.

"Sherri, what the hell happened?"

"Kodi just left me! How could he do that and be so selfish, Trent?" Sherri screamed hysterically into the phone. "Trent, I don't know what to do. Kodi is my life." She sobbed.

Trent was floored, "Sherri, don't cry. I'm going to fly down tonight. Ok."

He could hear Sherri sniffing over the phone attempting to get her emotions in check.

"Thanks so much. I need you here to help me and William get through this."

"What's happening?" Shia asked as soon as Trent disconnected the call.

"Kodi shot himself." He replied looking down at her.

Shia opted not to say anything in response to what Trent said. She personally wasn't affected either way. She felt as if the world was a better place without Kodi in it. Even though she still couldn't prove it, she felt in her heart that he had something to do with Leigh's disappearance and probably Remi's as well.

Trent was too busy rushing around to pack to notice Shia's silence.

"I'm heading out to DC tonight." He stopped packing to focus his attention on her, "You coming?"

"No." Shia felt bad about saying no to Trent, but between the two of them, there was way too much going on. She had to focus on somehow getting her boys back and finding Leigh and Remi. Everything was out of whack.

"No." Trent repeated as he went back to packing. Now he was irritated that after he had gone to D.C. for Shia, she wasn't willing to do the same for him.

Shia could hear the distance in his voice. "Baby," She said as she reached out and grabbed his arm to prevent him from packing; forcing him to focus on her.

"I want to go and be there with you, but I can't right now. I have to see the boys and work on getting them back Remi and Leigh are out there somewhere and I have to focus on that right now."

Trent knew she was telling the truth, but he'd wanted her to make the sacrifice.

"Yo, it's cool. I got this."

Shia felt bad, but she had to do what she had to do.

"I have to go, but please call me when you get there ok."

"Yeah, aight."

"Ok, don't forget to call me." Shia said blowing him kisses as she made her way out the door.

* * * *

Banging on Demetri's door, Shia was ready for any fight he tried to throw at her, but one thing she knew was that she was not leaving this spot until she saw her children. After five minutes had gone by with no answer, Shia banged on the door again with all her might. Demetri finally came to the door with fire in his eyes.

"What the fuck do you want?" he hissed at her.

"You know exactly what I came here for. Where are they?" Shia yelled in the hallway, trying to slip past him into the apartment.

"Get from out front my door before I have you removed for trespassing and violation of a court order."

"I'm not violating any order. Nothing says I cannot see my kids." Shaking her head, she gave him a look of disbelief, "I can't believe you told the state I abandoned my boys. You know I would never do that."

"It's obvious you did otherwise you wouldn't be standing at my door begging to see them."

"Honey, you ok?"

Shia smarted when she heard the vaguely familiar female voice speak in the distance.

"You have a woman around my children? Are you crazy?" She screamed.

Demetri backhanded Shia across her mouth so hard she fell to the floor. He finally had enough of her disrespect.

Shia tasted the blood in her mouth as she got up from the floor. She could already feel her mouth begin to swell around the gash. Like a mad woman, she ran full speed into Demetri like a football player going in for a hit. She kicked him in the knees and when he winced from the pain, Shia dug her nails into his eye sockets. She didn't care if he was never alive to see the light of day again.

Demetri wanted to kill Shia when her nails made contact with his eyes. In spite of the pain and barely being able to see, he raised his fist and punched her in her neck until she fell to the ground. Watching her wither in pain as she tried to breathe, he reached down, grabbed her arms and drug her body out of his door way and shut the door. He would see Shia in court.

* * * *

"You can stay with us in our hotel room is you want."

"No, thank you." Trent replied to Sherri. He had just arrived at National Airport and Sherri had picked him up.

"Thank you for flying down right away. They will be releasing his body over to the family tomorrow." Sherri wiped the tears from her eyes, "I can't believe he's gone. He just left me and William to fend for ourselves."

Trent had mixed emotions about the whole thing. He remembered the last time Kodi was in New York and stopped by his place. Kodi had told Trent that he was in some deep shit and didn't know how to get out of it. They'd had a few drinks and Kodi kept saying he should have never got involved with Sherri. And Trent hadn't argued with him. He'd told Kodi years ago to leave Sherri's crazy ass alone. He wouldn't be surprised if the ruling on the autopsy came back as a homicide instead of a suicide and that Sherri had actually murdered him, but that wasn't for him to decide.

"Where is William?"

"I left him with Phylicia back at the hotel. She flew down earlier."

Trent closed his eyes as he sat in the car waiting to arrive at their destination. Not only had his boy Kodi died today, now he had to deal with Phylicia. "Damn," he thought, "I just can't catch a break."

Sherri pulled up to the valet station at the Gaylord Hotel at the National Harbor and got out. Trent followed in her wake.

Stopping by the front desk to book his own room first. Getting his room key, he followed Sherri to the room she was sharing with Phylicia.

"Hey you two," Phylicia said as Sherri and Trent walked through the hotel door.

"Hey. Where is William?"

"Sleep. He lay down not too long after you left."

"Oh, ok. I'm a check on him real quick. Be back in a few."

"How are you?" Phylicia asked Trent. "I'm aight." Trent wasn't really up for the small talk he wanted to make sure Sherri and William were ok. The he needed to be left alone so he could grieve the loss of his homeboy, his ace, his friend.

"I've been having a tough time dealing with Khloe's death."

"Yeah, me too."

"Why didn't you call me? You know I'm here. We can get through this together."

"Yo P, I'm good. I'm dealing with it my way and I'm good."

"What y'all out here talking about?"

"Nothing. If all of you are good, I'm a head to my room. Goodnight."

Trent was happy to leave the ladies and head to his room. He just needed some alone time away from everyone to clear his head.

Returning to his room, Trent felt as if he didn't know whether he was coming or going. Not only did he have to come to grips with Kodi's death; P wanted to bring up Khloe's death. He was still having issues handling the sudden world of not having his little girl assumed anymore.

Walking over to the bar Trent took three shots of vodka. He needed something to put himself at ease. He wished Shia could come with him, but he knew that she was dealing with her own demons and it was selfish of him to ask her to come in the first place.

Sitting on the sofa, he stared like a zombie into space thinking about the good times he and Kodi used to have.

"Yo T, stop frontin and let's get some bitches."

"K, they not all bitches."

"Yeah, you right, but the ones that get blessed by the god usually turn out to be."

Trent lay back on the couch smiling at the memory. He was going to miss his homeboy.

Chapter Twenty-Three

"Your honor my client would never leave her children unattended."

"Yet, that's exactly what happened." The counsel for the plaintiff countered.

Shia stood in the courtroom with tears sliding down her face. She could tell by the judge's expression that he wasn't moved by anything her counsel was saying. She knew she wasn't going to get custody of her boys back today. Right now, she just hoped she would be allowed visitation. The way things were going, she couldn't be sure.

Shia cut her eyes over at Demerti and wanted to strangle him as he sat over there with his mouth turned up in a smug little smile. She now knew why women snapped and killed their husbands. If she could find a way to murder Demetri and get away with it, she would no doubt in her mind.

"My client has also suffered an assault at his house when the defendant arrived unannounced and attacked him when he wouldn't let her in."

"That is a bold faced lie your honor." Shia screamed, jumping up from her seat.

The judge banged his gavel on the table.

"Counsel, please keep your client in order."

"Ms. Cunningham you're going to have to stay seated and keep yourself composed." Her lawyer whispered to her in a warning tone.

"But he is lying. He struck me first." She furiously whispered back as she took a seat.

"That may be true but you don't want to come off disrespectful and irrational during this hearing. We're trying to get your children back remember?" Shia looked at him incredulously,

"Well if he's claiming I assaulted him, what do you plan to come back with to prove I didn't?" Shia asked him trying to keep her attitude in check.

"If you and your client are done. We would like to continue."

"Yes your honor. I would like to continue and start by saying that there is no proof of alleged assault and ask that to be stricken from the record."

"Sustained." The judge replied.

Shia smiled. Demetri really thought he was going to get away with this, but even if he won this battle, she knew the victory of the war would be hers.

"All rise." Shia and Demetri each stood with their respective attorneys.

"At this time, the court believes it is in the best interest of the children to leave then in the custody of their father Demetri Cunningham, with visitation granted to their mother Shia Cunningham every other weekend. We will reconvene in six months pending a review.

"Court adjourned."

Shia stood unfazed. She expected these turns of events. It would be okay. The war was only beginning.

* * * *

Glancing at the calendar in her kitchen Shia penciled the boy's visitation in for the following weekend. With the court hearing five days behind, her, she was now on a mission to get her babies back home.

Walking through her quiet apartment, she couldn't believe that she'd once complained about her sisters being in her space. Now with everyone gone, the place was empty. There seemed to be nothing she could do, yet so much needed to be done and unfortunately, for her so much was out of her control. Picking up the box of her mother's things that she had found, she went into the living room and looked through the contents again. Something was nagging her that she couldn't quite put her finger on.

Sorting through the love notes of her mother's many lovers she stopped when she came to the one she was seeking. Setting it on the couch, she retrieved her bag that she had taken to DC and pulled out the yearbook Ms. Carol had given her. Shia flipped through the book until she came to the page that held each of the senior's hand written messages saying what they were

Shia zoned in on the message one particular student had wrote.

"This has been an interesting year. College awaits me and I'm excited to see what becomes of my year at Howard University. I bid you all farewell as I exit this chapter and begin another. However, before I depart, I want to leave you with these words, "Greatness is achieved through great things, and great things are acquired because of amazing people, so do what you can to be an amazing person. Maryland by way of New York represent! ~Maxwell~"

Shia shook her head at the quote. How could someone change so much she thought.

Picking up the letter she had sat on the couch, she held it up to the signature in the yearbook. Though one was signed Maxwell and one with just an M. there was no denying that the same person had written both.

Shia dropped the letter on top of the book and covered her mouth with her hand in shear disgust. What kind of person would do something like this? She was married to and had children by the same man who was in love with her mother. Running to the bathroom Shia made it to the commode just in time to heave the day's contents of food out of her. Tears and vomit running down her face Shia knew she was a mess as she sat on the cold floor. She needed her sisters, her kids, a man, something because she was two seconds from losing the little peace of mind that she had left.

* * * *

Demetri was content in his world. The boys were off somewhere with his friend. He loved when they were gone, he hated them in his space all the time. He and Shia weren't even supposed to have kids. That had never been in the plan. She caught him slipping. He'd never planned on marriage her, but once he's gotten to know her he'd allowed himself to be human and have feelings again. With a smile like Shia's, it was more of an effort not to love her. He'd been caught up in his own game. Three years caught up and that's why things began changing. He hated who he had become and hated Shia for making him lose focus of his mission in life, but that was over now. He didn't need her anymore. His heart turned back to stone.

Glancing around his apartment that had the boy's toys everywhere he wondered how long he would be able to maintain this caring father act. He would prefer the boys to live with Shia, but he needed her to stay in a vulnerable position and keeping the boys from her while she was going through her sisters being missing was the best way for Demetri to keep the upper hand. She needed him right now, but he was no fool. He knew that Shia was sitting home strategizing the best way to get her boys back and Demetri was ready for anything that she could throw at him. He would one up her no matter what.

"We're back."

Demetri sighed. He had to find something to do with the boys so they didn't continually cut up his peace.

"Babe, where are you?"

"Yo." Demetri yelled from his back office.

"Why you hiding out in here?"

"Because I want to Phylicia, damn. What do you want?"

"I was just asking, damn."

Demetri rose out of his chair, "What did you say?"

Phylicia took a step back. "Nothing. I wasn't saying anything."

"I didn't think so."

"Avionne and I are about to leave."

"Where are you going? Why don't you keep the boys?"

"Because I have to go to DC. Kodi's funeral is tomorrow and I promised Sherri I would be back in time for it."

"I guess I'll have to keep them then."

"I mean, they are your kids. If you don't want them give them back to their mother."

"Now, you trying to tell me what I should be doing with my life. Is that it?" Demetri asked getting up in Phylicia's face.

Phylicia took another step back, "That's not what I was saying and you know it. I was only making a suggestion."

Grabbing her wrist and Demetri held tight to her pressure point.

"Until I ask, keep all suggestions to yourself okay," he said gripping her wrist harder until Phylicia thought she was going to pass out and then abruptly let go.

"I didn't mean any harm." Phylicia whined as she massaged her wrist in the spot that felt as if Demetri had tried to amputate if from her hand.

"You never do." Demetri said turning away from her to exit the office, "Get your child, and get out of here."

Phylicia watched as Demetri left the room, "He's going to get his. I'm a see to it," she thought to herself.

* * * *

"Hello, may I have an airline ticket to DC for tomorrow afternoon?" Shia asked the travel agent over the phone.

After she had gotten herself together and accepted what was and what needed to be, she knew that she would be okay. Her brain was slowly beginning to work again, but first things first; she needed to get to Trent. Tomorrow couldn't come soon enough.

Chapter Twenty-Four

After over a week in D.C. Trent was no closer to finding out anything about why Kodi would kill himself. They had buried his ace yesterday and he knew men weren't supposed to show emotion, but he'd grown up with Kodi. They were boys. He'd be lying if he said part of him hadn't been buried underground with Kodi.

"You holding up okay?" Phylicia asked softly walking into the hotel behind Trent. She could tell by his demeanor that he was hurting.

"Not really, but I'll be good."

"You sure? I can come up with you if you need the company."

"That's probably not a good idea. I'll be cool. See ya later." Phylicia watched as he got on the elevator and shut the doors without asking her if she was going up.

Trent entered his hotel room and shut the door. There was so much he couldn't and didn't understand. Looking down at the box Kodi's mother gave him. He wondered what it was. Kodi had left the box in his mother's custody with specific instructions to be given and opened by Trent should anything happen to him. Trent found it odd that Kodi had expected something to happen to himself. Just as Trent was about to open and search the box, a light tap came at his door. Putting the box on the floor by the bed, Trent looked out the peephole to see Phylicia standing there. He sighed with mild frustration.

Phylicia smiled up at Trent when he opened the door. She could tell that he didn't want to be bothered, but she didn't want to be alone tonight and figured why should she be.

"What's up?" Trent asked not wanting to let her in. He knew what Phylicia wanted and he didn't want any parts of it.

"I don't think you should be alone right now, so I'm going to entertain you."

Trent gazed into her eyes and parts of him could remember why he had fallen in love with her all those years ago.

Phylicia gloated on the inside. He was softening like he always did where she was concerned.

"I don't need to be entertained. I need to be alone."

"No you don't. If I leave you alone you're going to be in here driving yourself crazy with memories of you and Kodi."

Trent hated to let Phylicia see him hurting, but his emotions had taken over the last couple of months of his life and were whipping his ass.

"It's ok, baby. I'm here for you." Phylicia said attempting to pull Trent into a hug, but was interrupted by someone knocking on the door.

"You expecting company?'

"No," Trent replied moving away from Phylicia's failed hug attempt.

Trent was shocked after glancing through the peephole and realizing who was on the other side of the door. Suddenly, his spirit lifted and he was anxious to open the door.

"What are you doing here?" He asked after throwing open the door in excitement.

"Even though I'm going through hell at the moment, I didn't want to leave you to go through this alone." Shia said taking notice of Phylicia sitting in the room with a smug look on her face. "Though it seems you already have someone keeping you company."

"Oh," Trent said forgetting that Phylicia was still in the room," P just stopped by after the funeral to check on me. She's about to roll though."

Phylicia was appalled. Who the hell did Trent think he was just throwing her out like that?

"Hello, Phylicia." Shia broke the awkward silence in the room by being cordial, "Long time."

"Obviously, not long enough." Phylicia responded with a snide attitude. "Baby, I thought I was keeping you company." She said invading Trent's space trying to push up on him.

Trent politely moved away from Phylicia as Shia made herself comfortable in the room, by taking off her cardigan and removing her shoes.

"Thanks for stopping by P. I appreciate it." He held open the door so she could exit, "Have a nice evening."

"You're really throwing me out because she came here?"

"Yo P," Trent let out a tired sigh, "I'm not throwing you out. I said thank you for the company, but I'm a chill with Shy right now. Aight."

"Whatever nigga." Phylicia mugged Shia before exiting the room in a huff.

"What's up with her?" Shia asked.

"You know how P is. She doesn't mean any harm."

Shia rolled her eyes at his delusional statement. "Yes she does. Some people just never change."

"I don't want to talk about her. What really made you fly down here?"

"You." Shia said slowly removing her clothes. "I need you to help me forget just for a little while all the crazy shit I'm dealing with right now and I'm sure you could use a distraction as well."

The magnetic pull of their bodies is indescribable. Whenever in each other's presence, sharing the same space and air, reality ceased to exist, in the darkness, and running her hands down his sculpted back, Shia could feel every breath that Trent took. The closeness they shared was unimaginable. Everything about them felt so right, but was happening so fast. Was this how life was supposed to be?

Lovers tend to be in their own world, creating their own reality, relishing in it always ready and willing to justify it.

Consumed in her own thoughts, Shia was caught by surprise when Trent kissed her neck. Immediately moaning and seeking more of his touch, she was enchanted. The scent of him alone could make her body pulsate. Turning her face slightly so her lips could reach his, she kissed him longingly trying to memorize the shape and feel of the contours of his mouth. Everything about Trent excited Shia. The sound of his voice, with its deep, slow drawl and New York laced accented slang and the way his eyes roved over her body making her very aware of her womanly charms. As he brought his hands to the small of her back and gently began to massage her there, Shia's breath caught. She was becoming undone. She lived for these moments, the moments when Trent was caressing her and making her feel like the only woman in the world to him.

Trailing his fingers up her nude body, he brought his hands around to graze her erect nipples. Letting out a low, slow moan, Trent bent his head to capture one into his mouth. Audibly sucking in her breath and whimpering softly, Shia wanted to die. How could this one man make her feel like putty in his hands?

Slowly, but firmly guiding her down on the bed, Trent followed every motion of his hand with his tongue. With Shia now lying down, he was more able to explore the full length of her. Kissing underneath her breast, he slowly trailed his tongue to her belly button, where he could lick circle patterns. Gingerly lowering his kisses, Trent arrived at the bud he was seeking. Gently sliding Shia's legs further apart, he softly kissed her magical spot. Unable to contain herself, Shia's breathing quickened. Trent knew exactly what to do to excite her. Darting his tongue in and out of the parted lips that covered the flourishing bud he wanted to suck on, Trent grabbed Shia's hand, placed it to his head, and let her guide him to the place she wanted. Head firmly in her favorite spot, Trent sucked and licked Shia until she was nearly jumping off the bed. "Baby, please." Shia moaned breathlessly. That was his undoing. Not being able to hold back any longer, Trent let his tongue send her to orbit.

Recovering any sense of what was going on was hard, but Shia had to try. She had no idea how long she had zoned out after Trent had sent her to the moon. Turning her head, she could see him waiting patiently for her to regain her composure. Completely nude with his body looking like a Greek god, Shia noticed that his member was standing at full attention and ready for anything she had to offer. It's as if Trent's body was calling her name and who was she, not to answer its call.

Shifting slightly so she could be on top of Trent, Shia kissed down the length of his body until she found what she was seeking. Erect, posed and ready, Shia took all of Trent in her mouth and gently began to suck on his head. Licking small circles with her tongue, she slowly worked her mouth down the full length of him. She knew he liked it by the way he grabbed the back of her head and moved it and his body in sync with one another. Now saliva induced, Shia took both hands and began to massage up and down Trent's shaft. He moaned deeply as Shia sucked a little harder and increased her hand motions. From the jerks of Trent's body, she knew he was on the verge of cumming, flicking her tongue over the head again and continuing her swift hand motions; Shia smiled as she felt Trent's eruption filling up her mouth. Swallowing his savory reaction to her hand and tongue game, she knew he was satisfied. Lying on her back beside him, Shia felt Trent kiss her on the check and wrap his arms around her. Speaking softly he said, "You give that grown woman lovin' and nothing compares to that." Smiling to herself in the darkness, Shia wrapped her arms around Trent as well and they lay together as Shia fell asleep peacefully.

As Shia slept, Trent got up and retrieved the box Kodi's mother had given him. Unable to sleep even after Shia's good loving he decided to go through the contents to see if Kodi may have left him a clue as to why he had shot himself.

Opening the box, Trent could see that it held an envelope, a tape recorder, and a videotape. Trent played the tape recorder first.

"Aye yo, T, shit is crazy. A nigga just bout to hang it up. Seriously, the heat coming down fast and hard. It's my fault. I didn't have to get involved, but I did. I didn't know D was that damn crazy. Shit about to hit the fan. Watch your back T. They all involved in it. It's been years in the making. Phylicia used to be married to D. How we miss the radar on that shit? This shit is deep. D was messing with Shia Mom's my nigga. I don't have the whole story on that, but her parent's death was reopened from the cold case files and forensic could match cigarette butt samples w/D. I think he killed their parents and was on some revenge type shit to take out the whole family. I ain't know that shit at the time, but shit wasn't adding up so a nigga had to start investigating. Yo T, I ain't go experience fucking with a sociopath. Shit crazy. Sherri was on get back with Leigh ever since she took William from daycare that day. So, I help shortie out so she could finally say what she needed to say to Leigh, but T, they all tied up in this shit. D had Phylicia set up Sherri and me. Yo T, the shit gets crazier this nigga D is like a puppeteer. He's been setting all our asses up for years. He involved all of us so we wouldn't be able to take him down without taking ourselves down in this whole fucked up process. He played off our emotions. Whatever went down with him and Leigh's moms must have been some serious shit. Some evidence suggests an affair. His DNA was found on her body. My nigga do you understand what's happening? This psycho nigga on some get back shit. I don't think he planned on you and Phylicia hooking u and having a baby. You gotta watch that hoe, T. She knee deep in his shit. They a fuckin' team. He plans to take out the sisters one by one. Phylicia been breaking down telling Sherri bits and pieces of the story, but I still wouldn't trust her T. I don't care if the bitch having second thoughts or not..."

There was a screeching noise and the tape ended.

"What the hell was that?"

Trent jerked his head up looked towards Shia; he had no idea when she had woken up or how much she had heard.

"I'm not sure." He replied

Shia pulled the blankets around her as she rose out of the bed, to walk over and sit next to Trent on the sofa.

"That was Kodi's voice on that tape. Who is D that was messing with my mom and what does he mean he was helping Sherri with some get back plan?" Shia was visibly upset. "I need answers."

"Why you upset with me? I just listened to the tape myself." Trent responded trying to defend himself.

"Because if he's telling you this on tape, he's saying it like you should know some of this stuff." Shia looked at Trent expectedly. She knew he knew something.

"Aye Shy, calm down. I don't know where your sisters are or about some get back plan. All I do know for sure is I found out that Demetri was Phylicia's ex-husband the day Khloe was rushed to the hospital and he came there to pick up Avionne."

"And you didn't think it was a good idea to tell me that because...what?" Shia was shocked and hurt. Because you're already going through a lot. I didn't know how to break the news to you." Trent knew that was a weak excuse, but he honestly didn't know what to tell her.

"Speaking of which, how didn't you know he had another child? Phylicia had every other weekend to herself because she sent Khloe to me and Avionne to her dad."

Shia was not going to let Demetri or Trent make her feel like a fool.

"Fuck you Trent. My marriage may not have been perfect, but it worked for us. Demetri said he had out of town business every other week and I never questioned it, because he was doing that when I met him." Hearing those words out loud Shia did feel a little sheepish now. That excuse didn't hold water when you thought about it.

She suddenly began to smile, "I guess that sounds ridiculous huh." Shia looked over at Trent sheepishly.

Trent shrugged, "Nah just seems like you didn't care enough to find out if that was really what he was doing."

"Maybe Leigh was right after all. Maybe I never really loved Demetri; he was just something convenient to do that popped into my life at just the right time." Shia shook her head. "That seems so crazy now when I think about it." I never give Leigh the credit she deserves. She's my twin, why wouldn't I take her thoughts and opinions into consideration? I always talk about her and disregard her more. I would give anything to have her here with me. Anything."

Trent pulled her into a hug, not sure if he were comforting her or himself. Maybe the comfort was for each other since they both were living in a fucked up world at the moment.

Chapter Twenty-Five

Waking out of her sleep in a deep sweat, she didn't know what woke her. Glancing around the cold isolated room the best she could, she noticed the dimly lit overhead light swinging softly from side to side. Her hands and body were strapped down to a table and she was unable to move. Her mouth was taped, so she couldn't scream out. Trying her best not to panic, she willed her breathing to stay at a normal pace. She needed to think and in order to do that she had to remain calm. The last thing she remembered was...nothing. Breathing in slowly, she exhaled just as slow. Why couldn't she remember anything?

"Good you're awake."

She wanted to turn her head at the sound of the voice but couldn't. Hearing footsteps slowly coming her way, her breathing became rapid as she started to panic.

"Relax; I don't intend to hurt you if you tell me what you know."

The occupant of the menacing voice said as they stepped into her limited line of vision. Clothed from head to toe in a black hooded cloak, face covered by a mask, the figure brought something up to her forehead. Terrified, she anxiously turned her face away from what was in their hand, relaxing when she felt the cool cloth wiping away the sweat on her face.

"I told you, I don't intend you any harm."

"If I tell them what they want to know," she thought.

"I'm going to remove the tape, even if you scream, no one can hear you. Do you understand?"

Nodding her head slowly, she was beyond nervous. Where was she that even if she screamed no one could hear her?

Putting the cloth down, the mysterious cloaked figure slowly began to remove the tape away from her mouth.

Her eyes watered from the sting of the removal as she felt the little hairs around her mouth being individually ripped from her face.

"Why?" She asked in a voice dry and raspy from disuse that she didn't recognize.

"Why are you here?" The stranger asked. She nodded. Not ready to hear her own unidentifiable voice again. "Because you are the key." The stranger said moving out of her line of vision.

"The key?" She thought to herself. The key to what?

“Don’t worry it will all be apparent soon. Back to sleep you go.” The mysterious stranger said as they took a needle and injected medicine into Leigh’s veins sending her back into oblivion.

* * * *

Leigh felt groggy as she woke a short time later. The tape hadn’t been returned to her mouth, which she was grateful for. Hearing a faint moaning noise, Leigh moved her head as much as she could toward the sound. Even though it was extremely dark, Leigh would recognize her baby sister anywhere.

“Remi.” She whispered in a voice raspy due to non-use.

The figure nodded anxiously. Leigh sighed in relief. She could recognize that Remi’s hands and feet were bound and her mouth was covered with tape. Why hadn’t she been given any drugs? Leigh thought to herself. Since she’d been kidnapped this was the first time that she’d been awake this long.

Still strapped to the table Leigh wasn’t in a position to help Remi, she couldn’t even help herself, but she was happy to have her sister with her.

"Remi, you have to relax. You can still hop around. There has to be something in here that can cut through the rope around your hands and feet?"

Remi gazed around the room, there was nothing in there with her and Leigh except the table Leigh was strapped too. Straining through narrowed eyes, she was trying to see if the table had any sharp corners. Eyes widening at her discovery, Remi struggled to her feet and began hopping toward the table. She was almost in reach when she suddenly heard the sound of keys jingling in the distance. Panic stricken Remi awkwardly hopped her way back to her space on the wall, lay down on the floor and closed her eyes to appear as if she were sleep.

"What should we do with them?"

"Kill them."

Eyes still closed Remi began to have an anxiety attack when she heard the male voice. Her body began to tremble at the words, "Kill them."

"Are you sure? I never wanted or expected this to go this far."

"Who told you to have expectations?" The male voice asked.

Remi got the courage up to open one eye a slit wide and watched the man stick a needle in Leigh's arm. No wonder Leigh stayed half-delusional. They kept shooting her up with drugs. Remi wondered why she hadn't been drugged with anything and laid out on a table like her sister.

"No one. But with Kodi killing himself, we no longer have an inside connect with the police, so they're really going to be looking for them now and I don't want to be connected to murdering someone. Kidnapping them is bad enough, but murder? I can't." The female began to sob.

"I suggest you pull it together so you don't become a statistic like they are going too."

"I'm fine. It's just that this is so drastic."

"This is bigger than you and them. Let's go."

The female sniffed again as she looked in Remi's direction. "What about that one. You're not going to drug her?"

"No, I want her fully alert while I torture her sister to death." He replied as they exited the room.

* * * *

"He's crazy."

Phylicia sat across from Sherri eyeing her intently. She and Avionne had touched down in D.C. a little over forty-five minutes ago and now they were sitting in Sherri's new rental home since she had refused to return to the home she and Kodi had shared.

Phylicia shrugged. "Tell me something I don't know."

"Why you sitting over there all nonchalant like?"

"Because you not telling me anything new. And where do you get off saying words like kill over the phone?" You don't know if our phones have been tapped, if we're being followed or any of that. You need to tighten up and stop being so fuckin' emotional for one in your life."

Sherri jumped over the chair and snatched Phylicia up by her hair, "Who in the hell are you talking too like that?" Phylicia withered in pain as Sherri continued, "Bitch, watch your step. Please don't be fooled by the tears. You know me better than that, so *you* tighten up." Sherri spat releasing Phylicia's hair. Sherri knew she had mellowed out through the years, but she still had her crazy fighting ways about her and still didn't take kindly to being talked to in the tone Phylicia had used.

Phylicia looked Sherri up and down as she revealed the 9mm with a silencer attached that she had strapped to her back and pointed it at Sherri.

Sherri's eyes widened to the size of saucers. "That's why you flew out here so fast." She whispered, "I should have known. Someone as vindictive and evil as you are would take out your Mama if you had to."

"You're the weak link." Phylicia whispered back with tears spilling from her eyes, "You're like a sister to me. I love you."

"If you loved me, you wouldn't be pointing a gun at me. Why are you doing this?"

"Because, you left me no choice." Phylicia whipped some of the tears with one hand keeping the other with the gun trained on Sherri, "I'll take care of William. I promise. I'll let him know what an amazing mother he had."

"Phylicia, don't do this, he doesn't have to win." Sherri pleaded.

"He won't." Phylicia assured her as her tears continued to flow heavily from her eyes, "I love you Sherri. I really do."

"Phylic---" barely able to see from the tears nearly blinding her, Phylicia pulled the trigger cutting Sherri off mid word as the bullet went straight through her forehead and out the back.

Phylicia watched as Sherri's body hit the floor and blood oozed from her wound. Sitting on the floor beside her friend, Phylicia cried until her eyes were blood shot red and puffy. Right there on the floor next to Sherri's body Phylicia began to pray the children's prayer, "Now I lay you down to sleep. I pray your soul the lord to keep, since she died in your wake, I pray her soul for You to take. Amen."

Turning off all the lights in the house, Phylicia cleaned the blood around the room and from all around Sherri. Then she put plastic over Sherri's head to eliminate a blood trail as she dragged Sherri's body to her bedroom and pulled her up into the bed tilted her head on the pillow so the gunshot wound couldn't be seen and pulled her comforter up over her to give the illusion that she was asleep.

Going down the hall, she checked on the children to make sure they were still sleeping. Packing a few of William's things in Avionne's bag, Phylicia took everything down to the rental car she had picked up at the airport. After changing her clothes, she went back into Sherri's bedroom and got into bed with her. Setting her alarm for 5:30, Phylicia and the kids would head back to New York before day break.

* * * *

Remi couldn't believe her good fortune. They weren't going to drug her; unfortunately, she had to think of an escape for them otherwise their dead bodies would be left for the rats as dinner.

Remi stumbled to her feet. Keeping an ear open for any noise from the other side of the door, she hopped over the table Leigh was lying on and turned so her back was facing the table. Holding her taped hands to the sharp corner of the table Remi moved them back and forth willing the grey duct tape to tear. Just when she began to lose hope, she heard a small tearing sound. Suddenly anxious to be free Remi rubbed her hands against the corner of the table even faster. She breathed a sigh of relief as soon as she felt the tape give.

"Thank you Jesus." Was the only prayer she could get out, but she knew that it was enough.

Removing the tape from around her hands Remi sat on the floor so that she could take the tape from around her ankles. As soon as Remi was completely free of the tape, she touched Leigh's face. Remi could see she was breathing slow and steady. Making quick work of the ropes tied around her body Remi tried to stay conscious of how long this was taking. She had no idea when their kidnappers would be back to get them.

"Leigh, we have to get out of here." Remi tried lifting Leigh, but she was nothing but dead weight as she lay there in a drug-induced coma.

If Remi were the crying type that's exactly what she would be doing at this moment. Leaving Leigh lying on the table Remi instead focused on a way out of this hellhole. The last few days she was cooped up in the room with Leigh, she had taken in her surroundings. The door was the only logical way in or out of the room, but Remi had witnessed a rat crawl through a hole on the other side of the room. And her way of thinking was if a rat could crawl in then it was also crawling back out, which meant outside had to be close.

Scaling the wall, Remi found the rat hole and moved her hand around it. To her advantage or God's favor, the wall around the hole began to peel away. Forcing herself to go slow Remi gradually used her fingers to make the hole bigger without keeping too much noise unaware that by clawing at the wall she was setting off a silent alarm. It was a tedious process and her nails weren't likely to forgive her anytime soon from all the clawing she was doing, but she had no other choice. She and Leigh needed to get out of her as soon as they could. Remi had been listening during her kidnapped stay and noticed that she and Leigh seemed to mostly be there alone, especially at night, which made her wonder if they were being surveillance and this too was a set up. Even if it was, Remi couldn't be worried about it right now. She knew the type of evil they were up against and they stood a better chance trying to escape, because if they stayed, they would be goners for sure. Nothing more than a write up in the Murder Crime section of the newspaper.

Remi couldn't help but smile when a small ray if sunlight beamed through the hole. That's when the tears came. Tears of hope. She knew now that she and Leigh would be okay. Now all she had to do was find a way to wake Leigh.

* * * *

Phylicia dialed the number she was instructed to dial if anything unusual popped off. "My indicator went off on the way back to town. The sisters must be attempting to escape. The screen is showing the left wall is being tampered with."

"Damn. Why are you back in New York? Why didn't you go back?"

"I had the kids with me. What did you expect me to do, take them to the spot with me? They are six and seven years old. They're not babies. They would have been asking all kinds of questions."

"You're pathetic. I'll fly down and check, but if they've escaped by the time, I get there you better start saying your prayers and getting right with the Lord. Understand?"

Silence followed on the line.

"Damn it Phylicia, do you understand what the fuck I'm saying to you?"

"Yeah, I got it."

"Glad we understand each other." Were the last words spoken before the line went dead. Phylicia threw the phone against the wall; he would have his day with the maker, even if it killed her in the process.

Chapter Twenty-Six

Trent knew Shia was having a hard time dealing with everything. Ever since they had returned from D.C. three days ago, she had turned into a mute hermit. When they'd been at the hotel in D.C., he didn't get a chance to watch the video or see what was in the envelope that weighted the box because Shia had wanted to stay up comparing notes of what they knew.

Finally home relaxing, he figured this would be a good time to check everything out. He'd been hesitating, avoiding the box that sat on his coffee table for three days taunting him.

Kicking back on his sofa, he opened the box pulling out the tape recorder, video, and the envelope. Trent chuckled to himself, putting the items on the sofa. "A damn videotape." He thought to himself as he stood up, headed toward the storage room in his apartment, and prayed he hadn't thrown out his VHS when he'd moved years back. Shifting through various boxes in his storage room Trent was elated when his old VHS player from college surfaced. Hooking up the ancient video player to his 70' inch LED flat screen Trent laughed at how out of place it looked.

Once everything was hooked up, Trent put Kodi's tape in and sat back on the sofa to try to understand what his boy wanted him to see.

Trent watched as the tape opened up to surveillance of an airport. Immediately recognizing National Airport Trent sat up straight. Squinting his eyes he focused intently on the screen as he saw himself and began to panic. "What the hell?" He thought as he focused on what was happening at the airport. He could see someone who resembled Remi standing near one exit and Demetri standing at another; he continued to watch. Trent saw Leigh walk into view and enter the security check line. Reaching the front of the line, he watched as she was directed to get out the line and walk toward a side doorway. Trent saw Leigh go through the door and then the door shut behind her. Since the tape had yet to run out Trent kept a steady gaze on the screen making sure he didn't miss anything.

Looking on in astonishment Trent saw Kodi, Sherri, and Phylicia enter the tapes view. He'd had no idea that Phylicia and Sherri were at the airport that same day. Trent didn't understand what was happening. He remembered the cycle of events that had forced him into a position to be there the day Leigh was taken. All for the life of his daughter and he would do it all again to have her back with him. Trent continued to watch as first Kodi entered the room and then the two women following in a few seconds after him. Not too long after the women entered the room, the video cut off.

Turning the T.V. off with the remote, Trent opened the sealed envelope that was resting on his sofa.

"My nigga I'm done. Shit too crazy and out of hand. I never meant to disappoint you T, but even gods can have flaws. You were right; it was only a matter of time before some psycho shit went down with my crazy chick and me. I should have been left Sherri's unstable ass alone. The game is over T, that whack nigga talking about killing that girl. I can't be a part of that shit. I've done enough already. A package like the one I sent you is being sent to the lieutenant of police so he can know the deal, about a week after I do what I need to do. I love you man. PS: Marry Shia, she loves you, and she seems to be sane. I'll take a sane bitch over a psycho bitch any day. See you on the other side. One!"

Trent finished reading the note with a slight smile. He missed his homeboy. He wished that he could go back in time to when they were kids on the block just kicking it. Those was the good ole days. Now his boy was gone and it was just him

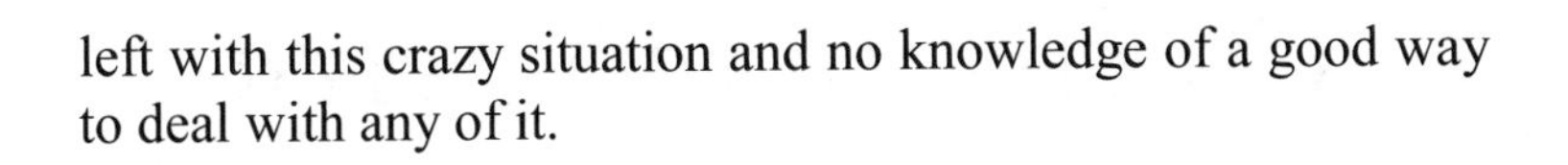

left with this crazy situation and no knowledge of a good way to deal with any of it.

Chapter Twenty-Seven

They were free by God's good grace and Remi's shear will. Remi looked down at Leigh who was still out like a light. "The girl must be on some damn good drugs." Remi thought. After digging through a wall for half the night to get a hole big enough for them to escape, Remi was sore and beat. But she didn't have time to focus on that because she'd had to figure out a way to drag Leigh's sedated ass through a dirt wall and through the trees. Remi was running on pure adrenaline. She needed Leigh to wake up and function before they were caught. Running as far away from here as they could was their only option.

"Leigh." Remi whispered kneeling down on the ground next to Leigh. "Lei, Lei I need you to wake up." Remi softly smacked both sides of Leigh's face, but nothing was working. Taking a deep breath, Remi raised her hand high and smacked Leigh across the face as hard as she could and separated the action until Leigh began to moan lowly.

Hearing the low noises, Remi began to shake Leigh.

"Please stop." Came the low raspy whispers.

"Oh my God thank you Lord." Remi pulled Leigh into a quick hug and then pulled back so she could get them moving.

"Lei," Remi watched Leigh's eyes as she struggled to focus.

"Mmmmmm, why are you yelling?" Leigh managed to squeak out.

"No time to explain." Remi stood up and grabbed Leigh's hand, "You think you can walk?"

Leigh's legs felt cemented to the ground. "I can try."

"Good."

Remi braced herself for Leigh's weight as she mustered up the energy to pull her to her feet.

"We have to run. I know you're groggy, but we have to get far away from this place. I don't know which direction to go through I feel lost."

"You don't recognize where we are? Come on Remi." Leigh whispered, "Look around you."

Remi's only concern was escaping she hadn't stopped to take in the scenery.

"Are you serious?" Remi looked at Leigh incredulously. "We don't have time to sight see. We have to go. They'll be back soon."

"Remi look around you, "Leigh said holding her ground.

Remi could tell Leigh wouldn't budge until she did what she was told. Sighing hard so Leigh would feel her frustration Remi observed her surroundings, and then sucked in a shocked breath when she began to recognize the space around her.

"Mommy and Daddy's house." She whispered.

"Yes." Leigh whispered behind her.

"This whole thing is personal. A lot deeper than me or you."

Remi looked up at the half charred housed and was overcome with sadness. She remembered all too well the events that had taken place here, and this experience added to that, but Remi never remembered the secret underground room they were in.

Without meaning to her mind whisked back to that fateful day when her world was forever changed.

"Remi baby, I'm going out for the night. Don't wait up."

Remi threw up in her mouth a little at her mother's suzary sweet voice. She didn't know who the lady thought she was fooling! Remi and her had both knew that her mother was going out to be with one of her many lovers.

"Whatever." Remi mumbled under her breath.

"What you say darling?"

"Nothing Mother. Have fun." Remi recited sweetly

"I'll try my best."

"I'm sure." Remi thought.

Remi had gone to bed shortly after that only to be awakened around midnight to the hushed whispers of a heated argument outside heard through her open bedroom window.

"Just leave him. I can give you a better life than anything he can offer you."

"No. You knew this was just a fling. It was never my plan to leave my family."

"You don't need them. I can give you a better family. I have a child of my own. Baby please."

"No. I'm ending this tonight before either of us gets hurt. I shouldn't have let it go on this long. It's my fault blame me."

"I do blame you. If you won't have me, you're choosing no family at all. I won't live without you."

"I don't love her anymore. I love you."

"This is crazy. I'm not dealing with this any longer. I know my husband is waiting up for me."

"Be real with yourself. You don't love him."

"You're right; I don't, but he loves me and I don't want to keep disappointing him. I have to go."

"I beg you to reconsider."

"I won't good night and good bye."

"You'll regret this," were the last words Remi heard before a car pulled away from the house. All Remi could do was shake her head. Her mother and her many boyfriends, how disgusting.

After tossing and turning for nearly an hour unable to sleep, Remi rose out of bed, throwing some clothes on and climbed out her bedroom window. She needed to go for a walk, something she did often at night to clear her head.

Walking around her neighborhood, she wished her sisters were here. Shia had left for the weekend to visit Leigh and Remi was left behind because her mother thought New York was to fast a city for a teenager without adult supervision. She had specifically pointed out that her sisters were adults, but all her mother said to that was, "They don't count."

Remi didn't think that was fair but whatever, she only had a few years left and then she could be out.

Enjoying her walk, Remi journeyed back to her street to find it lit up like the fourth of July. There were fire trucks and ambulance's everywhere. Remi wondered what was going on, that is until she got close enough to her parent's house to realize that's where all the emergency vehicles were because the house was sitting in a ball of flames. Heart beating a million miles a minute Remi took off running only to have the fire fighters stop her before she could get close to the burning house.

"Miss you can't go near the house."

"My parents are in there." Remi screamed trying to break through their hold.

"Miss you have to calm down and stay back."

A female officer approached Remi.

"I'm sorry; your parents didn't make it." Remi heard that statement in a trance-like state.

"No, that can't be true." Remi whispered.

"I'm so sorry sweetie. There was nothing anyone could do to save them. They were pronounced dead upon the medic's arrival."

"The officer gave Remi a hug, "Is there someone you want me to call so they can be here with you?" She asked pulling out her phone.

Taking the phone from her Remi dialed Shia's number.

"Hello?"

"Shy you gotta come home now."

"Remi, what's wrong?" When Shia said those words, Remi broke down and she couldn't stop the tears from falling.

"Something terrible has happened. You have to come home right now. You have to. I need you. I don't know what to do."

"Ok, ok, baby sis, slow down. Try to tell me what's wrong."

"Mommy and daddy..."Remi's voice trailed off as she watched the firemen dose the last reminders of the fire.

"Mommy and Daddy what?" Remi didn't hear Shia's whisper though her haze of disbelief.

"It wasn't till Shia screamed Remi into the phone that she realized she was still on the phone.

"Are dead." She said in a calm voice of finality and acceptance and hung up on Shia because she needed to clear her head.

"Thank you for letting me use your phone." Remi said politely to the counselor handing her phone back to her.

"No problem sweetie. Let's get you out of here.

"I'm okay; please let me stay until this is over."Remi was fine now a calming had washed over her.

"You're not ok honey. You're going into shock."
The officer placed her arms around Remi, guided the teen to her car, and transported her to the station, where Remi remained until Shia and Leigh came to get her.

"There is a secret passageway underground remember?"

Remi tuned back into her conversation with Leigh as if she's been listening the whole time.

"Why didn't we ever knock down this eye sore?"

"Huh?" Leigh was confused. She'd been trying to figure out an escape route.

"The house, we own this land, why didn't any of us think to knock this house of misery down?"

Leigh gave her a forlorn look. "I'm not sure. I guess living in New York offered us the freedom of not having to deal with it."

Now Remi was disgusted by even being here. "Let's get out of here. I can't stomach this place anymore."

"Too bad because you're not going anywhere."

The sisters turned in unison at the sound of the voice that was all too familiar to them then looked at each other with twin looks of horror at the realization they'd been caught.

Chapter Twenty-Eight

Waking up in a hot sweat, this was the first time in months that Shia could feel Leigh. The last few days she hadn't been eating or sleeping well. She was privy to a lot of information and not enough at the same time. She couldn't just go to the police with a tape recording of Kodi's voice on it. There was no way to prove it was actually him or that anything he'd said held any validity to it.

Shia glanced at the clock when her phone began to ring. She felt dread enter her bones. Her phone never rang at three in the morning.

"Hello." She tentatively answered on the third ring.

"Yo. You not gonna believe this shit."

Shia was on the edge already, what else could possibly go wrong.

"I just got notified by Kodi's mother that she stopped by the house to check on Sherri and William because she hadn't heard from them in a couple of days and found Sherri lying in bed with a gunshot wound to the head yesterday."

"You are not serious. She committed suicide too?" Shia asked curiously.

"I'm not sure. The police are investigating. They think it may be a homicide because William is missing."

"Oh my God. That poor baby."

"Yeah, the police have issued an Amber alert for him. They're doing double time on this one, especially since Kodi was an officer in D.C. They have issued an alert here as well since he is from New York and William could have been brought here. It's all over the news."

Shia cut the T.V. on as Trent continued to speak and sure enough she saw little William's face pop up with all his physical information.

"This is craziness."

"I know." Trent responded, "I don't know how Phylicia is taking any of this. When I tried to get into contact with her the voicemail picked up."

The sound of Phylicia's name made Shia's skin crawl.

"What to hear something weird? Right before you called, I woke up because I could feel Leigh. I know that may sound strange to you, but she's my twin. I needed to feel her. It means she is alive."

You got all that from waking up out your sleep?" Trent asked not really believing her.

"Yes! It's a twin thing. You wouldn't understand anyway."

"You're right. I wouldn't. I'm a hit P one more time and see if I can reach her."

"Okay. Call me back later and let me know what's what."

* * * *

"Oh shit!" Remi thought as she stared into Demetri's face.

Demetri trained his gun on Remi and Leigh, "Did you think you would just walk out of here and I would allow it?"

Neither of the women replied. They were stuck. They both knew if they tried to run, he would shoot them.

Remi finally broke the silence, "Why are you doing this to us? We never did shit to you."

"Your mother did enough, blame her." Remi had the stuck face.

"Our mother has been dead for years. You didn't even know her."

"Yes he did. He was one of Ma's boyfriends." Leigh interjected.

"What?" Remi said turning to face Leigh, unafraid for the moment. But Leigh was like a woman possessed.

"Isn't that right Maxwell?"

Demetri's eyes clouded over. "Fuck you and that evil bitch. The world is better off without any of you." Demetri went to pull the trigger and two bangs rang out.

Remi closed her eyes in anticipation of the bullets pelting he skin, but was surprised when she felt nothing and heard a thud on the ground.

Peeping one eye open Remi saw Demetri's unmoving body in a heap on the ground. Leigh and Remi were completely astonished to see a masked figure standing behind Demetri holding a smoking 9mm.

"The world is much better off without him. Don't you think? Fuck him." The masked person said in a disguised mechanic like voice.

Leigh and Remi had no idea what to expect at this point. Were they going to be shot next? They wondered.

"Relax; I'm not going to shoot either of you." As if reading their minds. "You're not the one I'm looking for." And the gunman turned and ran from the yard.

"What the hell just happened?" Remi asked Leigh.

"Girl, I have no idea." Leigh pulled Remi into a hug, "I love you baby sis. Thank you for not leaving me. It almost cost you your life." Remi thought she would faint when she saw the tears in Leigh's eyes. Leigh never showed emotion.

"Awww. I will never leave you. Life, death situation or otherwise. I love you too. We sisters are all we have left."

"You speak the truth miss. Let's go home. We'll call the police from there to report everything."

"After you." Remi bowed as Leigh led the way.

* * * *

Shia hadn't been able to return to sleep after Trent had phoned her. The hour was steadily inching toward eight a.m., and she was still in the bed. A faint clicking noise brought her upright in her bed. She could hear movement. Shifting her blankets to one side of the bed Shia cautiously put both feet to the floor and retrieved the Swiss army blade she kept on her nightstand. Gradually making her way to her bedroom door Shia listened carefully. It sounded as if the footsteps were coming closer to her. Body fitted to the wall like a glove. She waited patiently for the intruder to enter her doorway so she could initiate the assault before they got to her. The door creaked open and Shia went into full attack mode, blade swinging.

"OH SHIT. STOP!" A female voice that sounded like Leigh screamed out in pain once Shia's knife collided with her skin.

"Shia stop it's us! Your sisters!"

Shia didn't stop swinging until the word sisters registered in her psyche. "Huh?" She was confused as she walked over to her nightstand and cut the light on and saw Remi and Leigh standing in front of her. "How are you here?" She asked in a state of confusion, "What?" Then came the water works as she dropped the knife and smothered both of her sisters in a hug.

"You crazy heifa." Leigh whispered returning her embrace, "You cut me chick, and I'm half bleeding to death." She said holding her arm trying to stop the bleeding, "I'm pressing charges on your ass in the morning." Leigh said with a slight smile, slight grimace.

"Oh God Leigh, I'm so sorry." Shia yelled behind her as she ran to the medicine cabinet in the bathroom to retrieve medical supplies to tend to Leigh's wound.

After Leigh was all bandaged up the sisters sat together on Shia's king-sized bed.

"How in the world did you two get here? What happened to you? Where have you been?"

"Where do we begin?" Remi asked with slight laughter illuminating her features in an attempt to keep the mood light.

"At the beginning. Leigh what happened the day you vanished from the airport?"

Leigh shook her head, her mind still reeling from all the events that had taken place in the past few months. Shrugging as she looked at Shia, she filled her in on the suspicions she'd had about Demetri and what had led her to investigate him after seeing information that was left in her mother's box.

"I knew he couldn't be trusted Shy. I just knew it. My gut is never wrong. I just needed solid proof so you could know that my concerns were valid. Some how he got wind of what I was doing because at the airport, I was taken to a back room for what I thought was a routine security check, but turned out to be my kidnapping plan."

Leigh looked at them near hysteria, "I thought that kind of thing only happened in the movies. Anyway, they take me back and all I remember before I woke up in a dark room strapped to a table was that Kodi, Sherri, and Phylicia were there."

"Wait, come again…" Shia paused, "Sherri, Phylicia, and Kodi had something to do with this?"

"And Demetri." Remi chimed in. That dude is evil."

"I'm just so glad you're both here alive and okay." Shia said turning to Remi, "And what happened to you? I go away for one weekend to come back to you gone and a hand-written note by you saying I abandoned my kids. When I get back, Demetri has temporary custody of them. I had to go to court and everything. He still had them."

"Not anymore he doesn't. That nigga was the worse. I'm sorry Shy, but he had a gun to my head. I had no choice. It was either my life or let him have the boys until you could get back to sort it all out. So, I let him have the boys. Then he told me I had to fly out with him to D.C. to meet up with Leigh. We drop down in D.C., and then I remember waking up in the same room as Leigh."

"So, how did you two get back here? They just let you go?" Shia asked.

Leigh and Remi looked at one another as Remi answered Shia's question. "We escaped, and then got caught." Remi told her.

"That doesn't make sense. If you'd gotten caught you couldn't be here."

"Well, that's true and false."

"I'm confused." Shia replied.

"We did escape, but once we realized where we were, old emotions about the place overcame us."

"Where were you?" Shia asked.

"Mommy and Daddy's place."

"What?" Shia whispered, "You two were there the whole time?" Shia couldn't believe it. Never in a million years had she thought about checking her parent's old house for her sisters. None of them was back to the property since their parent's murder.

"The whole damn time. Shoot, I didn't know either. There's like some underground cellar down there that we knew nothing about." Leigh said adding to the conversation.

"So, we were there when Demetri strolled up behind us with a gun talking about the world was better off without any of us."

Shia joined them in ending the sentence. It was Remi and Leigh's turn to look at Shia in bewilderment, "How did you know that?" Remi asked.

"Because after Kodi killed himself, he left a tape recording giving Trent all the details of what went down."

"Kodi killed himself?" Leigh whispered.

Shia nodded yes, "And Trent called me earlier this morning and told me they found Sherri lying dead in her bed with a gunshot wound to the head."

"This is some crazy stuff going on. I can't wrap my brain around Kodi killing himself." Leigh said mostly to herself in shock.

"You'll never guess who else is dead," Remi smugly blurted out, "Demetri!" she exclaimed. "Someone shot him and let us go free." Remi explained. "This has been the craziest shit I've ever gone through in my life.

A thought suddenly dawned on Shia, "If Demetri is dead, then where are my boys?" She asked as the concierge buzzed her apartment intercom, “Ms. Cunningham, you have a visitor from Child Protective Services. Would you like me to send them up?”

“Yes, Malik that would be wonderful. Thank you.”

“You’re welcome Ms. They’re on the elevator now.”

Shia hit end on the intercom then ran to the front door throwing it open. She watched a chicly dressed woman who must be the social worker walk towards her with her boys in tow.

“Hello Ms. Cunningham. I’m Olivia McGowan.” She introduced herself as she extended her hand for Shia to shake.

“Yes ma’am.”

“I’m here to bring your boys to you. It seems as if their father left them with the nanny who left them alone because Mr. Cunningham had neglected to pay her. A neighbor heard them crying all night and finally called us. So, I have instructions to return them to you.”

“Oh bless you!” Shia cried as she fell to her knees and scooped her boys up into a heartfelt hug. This was an amazing morning. She had her sisters back and now her boys. She saw out of her peripheral; the social worker crept away and left the family in privacy.

Chapter Twenty-Nine

"Hello." Phylicia answered her cell on the first ring when Trent's name flashed across the screen.

"Hey P. You sitting down?"

"Not really. I'm en route. Do you need me to sit down?" Phylicia asked as she walked across the parking lot back to her car after dropping William and Avionne off for their first day at summer camp.

"Yes."

When Phylicia reached her car, she sat in the driver's seat and waited. "Okay, I'm sitting. What's up?"

"They found Sherri murdered in her house last night. Kodi's mother called and told me. They also can't find William. He's missing, so an Amber Alert has been put out for him. It's been all over the news."

Phylicia heard that last part and began to panic.

Trent mistook Phylicia's silence for sadness. "You ok P? I'm sorry I had to break the news to you the way I did, but I wanted you to hear it from me first."

"No, no. It's cool. I'm fine. Thanks for letting me know." Phylicia said as she got back out the car and reentered the kid's camp building. "I have to go. I'll holla at you later." She disconnected Trent's call. Gathering William and Avionne's things, she retrieved the children and headed home.

"God mommy, when is my mommy coming to get me?" William yelled from the back seat, while he sucked on a lollipop loudly.

"Soon baby." Phylicia lied to him.

"Mom why did you make us leave camp? We just got there." Avionne stated as she too sucked on a lollipop.

"We are going home. You guys get to spend the next couple of days with me." She told them turning the car radio up to drown out any more questions they may have.

* * * *

Trent was worried about Phylicia. Once he had told her about Sherri's death, she had hung up so abruptly. He knew how tight they were and hoped Phylicia wasn't beating herself up about what happened. He also wanted to speak with her about the videotape Kodi had sent him and find out why she was also on it.

"What's up babe?" Trent said into his phone after it vibrated in his hip.

"My sisters are home!" Shia sang into the phone.

"Yeah? Just like that, they're home."

"Yeah, just like that boo." Shia couldn't believe how calm he was being about the news of her sisters, "And I have my boys back. Demetri was killed in D.C."

That news stopped Trent cold. "Something ain't right." Trent said more to himself than to Shia.

"What do you mean?"

"There have been too many killings at the same time within the circle of people we know. Kodi killing himself was one thing, but now Sherri and Demetri. Doesn't that seem strange to you?"

"Not really." Shia replied, "Sounds like a bad case of karma to me. Everyone who was involved is getting exactly what they deserve."

Shia couldn't understand where Trent was coming from. She hadn't heard about a recent killing or death so far that she felt wasn't justified in some manner by the actions those individuals had chosen to take.

Trent understood where Shia was coming from, but he was worried about Phylicia and he knew Shia wouldn't understand.

"I hear where you're coming from Mami. Listen, I gotta roll. I'll hit you later. I'm glad your sisters are home safely." He hung up without waiting for a reply. He needed answers because things were not adding right and he felt there was a strong possibility that Phylicia could provide him with the necessary information to fill in the holes.

Pulling up to Phylicia's unannounced Trent parked and entered her building. Knocking, he waited for her to open the door. He'd peeped her car outside and knew that she was home.

Phylicia panicked when she heard a knock at the door. She was not expecting company. She'd made the kids lay down for an afternoon nap so that she could have some time to think and figure things out. Picking up her 9mm and placing it inside her pants at the small of her back, pulling her shirt over it, she made her way to the door. Looking out the peephole Phylicia breathed a sigh of relief when she saw Trent standing on the other side of the door. Taking the gun and placing it on the side table Phylicia opened the door.

"Hey." She said with genuine happiness. The only time she was ever happy in her life was when Trent was around and a part of her life.

"Yo, what's good? You aight?"

"Yes." She beamed, throwing herself into his arms for a hug while trying to sneak a kiss.

Trent accepted the hug, but turned away from the kiss. He knew this game all too well and wasn't willing to play it with her this time.

"Yo P, chill." Trent looked at her through guarded eyes, "I just came to check on you."

"Thanks for checking. Have a seat. Have a seat." She motioned to her sofa.

"Kodi left me a copy of the airport surveillance video from the day Leigh disappeared. You and Sherri were on it." Trent said jumping right into his real purpose for coming over, not wanting to waste time on small talk.

Out of all the things Trent could have said, Phylicia wasn't expecting that.

"Umm." She began not sure of what to say. Trent had really caught her off guard with that statement and she couldn't fabricate a lie when put on the spot like this.

"That's so crazy." She said in-between nervous laughs, "That we were all at that airport on the same day at the same time….ain't that something?"

"Aye P, cut the crap okay. You know something." Trent watched her every movement. The way she kept darting her eyes around the room was even beginning to make him nervous. "Why were you there that day? Were you involved in Leigh's disappearance?"

"Shit, I'm the reason the bitch could go home." Phylicia didn't feel like faking it any longer. She didn't care what Trent thought. She loved him, but if he became a problem, she would handle him the same way she did Demetri.

Trent was confused. "What does that mean?"

"It means that I don't understand why you want to have this conversation."

"Why didn't you tell me that you used to be married to Demetri?"

"Oh, so that's what this is about. Why would it matter who I was married too? It's in the past."

"Demetri and I grew up together. Did you know that?" Trent asked ignoring her question.

"What?" Phylicia was genuinely shocked. She'd had no idea that Demetri and Trent had grew up together. "That can't be possible he told me he used to live in Maryland and when he moved to New York, he changed his name from Maxwell to Demetri. I just liked Maxwell better and called him by that anyway."

"He's a liar Phylicia. He played all of us."

"That's where you're wrong. He didn't play me. If my memory serves me right I was dating you while I was married to him." Phylicia gave Trent the dumb look.

"You not fooling me P. He was having an affair with Shia and Leigh's mother in Maryland. That's why you started seeing me. You were on some get back type shit except your husband didn't care. I don't know why he married you, because according to the letters that Shia has from her mother who Demetri wrote, he was in love with Alycia….their mother."

Every word Trent spoke was hitting Phylicia like a ton of bricks because he was right. She'd always known that Maxwell was in love with another woman. He'd all but told her when they'd first begun dating, but Phylicia didn't care. She'd thought she could make him forget about anyone else, because her love could be enough for the both of them. She'd been sadly mistaken.

The first time Maxwell had hit her; her love for him began to diminish. The second time he'd almost killed her after insuring she end up in the hospital causing her to miscarry their first baby. He hadn't cared, one way or the other, when he had found out. There was no emotion to be found in him. That's when the love she'd once had for him fizzled and died. She no longer gave a damn after that.

Soon after that incident, she had gone to the museum to clear her head and relax, because living in an unhappy marriage was all but strangling her to death. She'd been minding her business when her purse accidentally dropped to the ground when out of nowhere a very handsome Trent had stopped to help her retrieve her items off the floor. She'd been attracted to him, no doubt, but she had still wanted to respect the fact that she was married. That is until a few weeks later when he'd all but lost his mind and beat up for no apparent reason, except he couldn't be with the woman he really loved because it seemed like she wouldn't leave her husband. After that Phylicia was completely done. She'd called Trent for a date and had a fantastic time. He'd shown her what it was like to have a man really love you. She'd never divulged any information, thinking it was unnecessary. She had explained to Maxwell, she couldn't do this pretend marriage anymore and moved her and her things in with Trent. Those were the best months of her life. Then one day she'd stopped by her old house with Maxwell retrieve some of the things that she'd forgotten. She had expected to be in and out, but Maxwell was there in a state of self-pity and drunkenness. That was the night her husband raped her braced on the kitchen wall with his hand around her neck all but shutting off her air supply. That was the final straw, so she thought until she found out a few weeks later that she was pregnant.

Not sure whose baby it was, Phylicia had kept everything to herself and let Trent think it was his. Trent was beyond excited and Phylicia wouldn't have told him anything except her conscience was getting the best of her and she'd finally broken down and told him she was married and there was a fifty-fifty chance the baby could be her husband's. Trent was livid. That was the end of their relationship. She hadn't told him about the rape not wanting to relive the events aloud.

"You're half right." Phylicia responded to Trent. "Except I wasn't on get back when you and I started dating you. My marriage to Maxwell was already over by that point. It's irrelevant now. That bastard is gone now. The world is much better off without him in it. He can't hurt anyone else or force anyone into helping him hurt anyone else."

Trent watched the pure hatred exhibited on Phylicia's features.

"You killed him didn't you?" Trent asked more so to himself than to her. That's when he noticed the gun positioned on the stand next to the door.

Phylicia followed his gaze to her weapon. "He deserved to die. He was an evil person. Destroying lives for the sole reason that he couldn't be happy with the woman he loved."

"And you think you're different? You almost destroyed my life until I met Shia."

Phylicia snorted, "What is it about her that causes men to flip out? First you, then Maxwell....I mean how is that even possible?"

"She's amazing." Trent replied without hesitation. She has a great heart and I love her."

"No, you don't. You just think you do."

"I really do P."

"God mommy? Can I see my Mommy now?"

Phylicia's eyes widened in horror. She'd forgotten all about the children napping in the other room.

William's little eyes lit up when he saw Trent. "God daddy!" He gushed, "What you doing here? You're going to take me back to see my mom?"

Trent's mind was blown as he looked over at Phylicia unable to answer William's question for the time being.

"It was you?" Phylicia knew exactly what he was stating that she that killed Sherri. Nodding with tears escaping her eyes, Phylicia still was choked up about it. It may not seem like it, but she had loved Sherri.

"She was the weak link." Phylicia whispered, "She was going to send all involved to jail. I could see it in her eyes."

Trent shook his head, "All involved? P this is crazy. What were you thinking?"

"William, go back in the room with Avionne. It'll be snack time shortly."

"Okay." William said running back to the other room momentarily forgetting he didn't get an answer to when he'd see his mother.

"I need answers P. That's why I came over here. Maybe I can help you."

"No one can help me. It's all going to be over soon. No one can take back everything that happened. No one."

Chapter Thirty

Trent didn't want to push Phylicia, but he needed to coax answers out of her.

"What happened?"

Gazing deep into Trent's eyes she could see he still cared. Maybe he was just the person she could talk to and he really could help her.

"Maxwell murdered both their parents. I believe that's when he went off the deep end. He stopped caring about everything after that. That's why he granted me a divorce. I thought that would be the end of it, but then not too long after he was dating Shia."

"Why didn't you go to the police? You're a lawyer. Aren't you supposed to help uphold the law?"

Phylicia shrugged indifferently. "Wasn't my business or my problem. I was done with him. Why drag myself into further involvement with him?"

Trent wasn't completely convinced by her answer, but allowed her to continue without interruption.

"Even though he was dating Shia, I didn't know at the time that she was Alycia's daughter. Then he decided to marry Shia and I thought even better because now she was out of your life." Phylicia stated looking at Trent, "I really thought that he had moved on and was truly happy. Then one morning not too long ago he calls me and says, "Here's the plan." He wants to kidnap one of the sister's and make Shia emotionally unstable and unfit as a parent. He gives me no choice in the matter. Pulls a gun on me and tells me if I don't do what he wants me to, that he will kill me. So at that point, I'm all in. I know what he's capable of so we fall into a routine. I begin treating him as if we're married again, even though I hate his guts. I value my life more. Everything started to become undone when Shia began retracing Leigh's steps trying to figure out what happened to her and you were with her. I believe that's when Kodi began to panic about his involvement in the situation. I'm guessing the consequences for cops gone bad could be pretty severe, which is why he shot himself to make it all end. Leaving you the unedited surveillance video must have been his way of coming clean. Anyway, Sherri began to buckle under the pressure and called me spazzing out because the plan changed from merrily kidnapping them to killing them. Maxwell told me to get rid of her when he saw she could no longer handle what was happening. Every time she went to administer Leigh's drugs to keep her pretty much in a vegetable state on the table. She was becoming more and more hesitant. Sherri would have ratted everyone out. So I flew down and did what I had to do, but she will always be my sister in spirit."

Trent couldn't believe what he'd just heard. Phylicia gave it to him straight.

"So why kill Dem-Maxwell?" Trent corrected himself, "If y'all were in this together."

"We were never in it together. I did what I had to do to save my life. When I told him the girls were escaping, his reaction to me quote unquote allowing them to was the last straw. I flew back down and blessed the sisters with the gift of life. A life for a life. I took his and allowed them theirs. It's all over now."

"Except for one problem, there is an Amber Alert out for William. You can't be seen anywhere with him." Trent pointed out.

"Yeah, I know. That does pose a bit of a problem, but I'll figure out something."

"Why not give him to Kodi's mother since Sherri doesn't have any family."

"I can't just walk him to her house Trent. That would tie me to Sherri's murder."

"So why not turn yourself in?" Trent asked softly.

"Are you crazy!" Phylicia yelled beginning to think it was a mistake to tell Trent the complete story. Her love for him had clouded her judgment. "You're not going to turn me in are you?" She asked him as she mentally calculated the distance to her gun.

Trent knew this wasn't the time or place. He'd get further with Phylicia by playing the game her way for the time being. William would have to stay put until things could be figured out.

"Sorry P, your secret is safe with me. I was only offering a solution to your predicament."

"No solutions needed. I'll figure it out myself."

"Aight." Trent responded.

* * * *

With the boys back in their rightful place with her, Shia's last couple of weeks was great. There was no funeral or memorial service for Demetri. As far as Shia was concerned good riddance to him, she wished she knew who had killed him. She would thank them personally for doing what she was unable to do.

Having Remi and Leigh home was a bonus. The two of them were inseparable these days. Both had opted not to go to the police about the situation they had merely had the missing persons reports lifted and Shia had respected their decisions not wanting them to have to deal with more than they wanted to. She wasn't a fool though. She knew continuing to date Trent was eventually going to drive Phylicia over the deep end, so she constantly stayed on guard for the unknown, whatever that was and what was to come.

These days the sisters were doing their best to get past the evilness that had claimed their lives for the last few months and put it all behind them.

"Shy, what you think about those adoption papers in Ma's box? You think we should look into it and see what's up?"

"I'm not really interested, but I you want to me can ask around." Shia answered Leigh. After everything they went through, the idea of hunting down their real parents wasn't appealing to her at the moment.

"I'm with you. I don't really care." Leigh looked at her with a question in her eyes, "You think we should tell Remi?"

"No." Shia replied without hesitation. "She's been through enough. Let's just let it be. What she doesn't know won't kill her."

"We should destroy the documents to make sure this never comes back into play." Leigh suggested.

"I second that." Shia agreed.

"Done." Leigh said retrieving the documents and burning them.

In her room, Remi was dealing with her own demons. Demetri ruined her life. There was no way she could ever tell Shia or Leigh about the daily rape sessions that had taken place with Demetri. The thought disgusted her every time it crossed her mind. She bathed no less than fifteen to twenty times a day in the hopes of somehow washing the filth of each encounter off her. But it never was enough. She had to fight this demon and beat it and she knew she would have to fight it alone.

Chapter Thirty - One

"Will you marry me?" Shia stared at Trent in a state of shock.

"Huh? Where is this coming from?" They were at dinner enjoying a 'post war' date if you will and she was completely taken off guard by his question.

"Marry me." Trent said holding onto her hand. "This past year has taught me that I can't possibly live one more day without you as my wife."

"Seriously? What makes you think that it will work out any differently than it has any of the other times?"

"Life. I'm more appreciative of everyone now. Having Khloe in my life and then taken out of it has taught me a lot."

"I'm not sure I want to jump into another marriage."

"You never really loved him, be honest with yourself and with me." Trent said to her. "I want you to be my wife and give me a pretty little girl who looks like you."

Shia was hesitant, "I don't know. I love you, there's no question about it, but I just don't know if I can do the whole marriage thing again." She stared into Trent's eyes. She knew he was serious and that it was real. She also knew she loved this man and they were stronger for the past they shared.

"Ok." She said with a smile, "I'll marry you. Let's try to keep it drama light." She laughed.

Trent caught her up in an airtight hug and refused to let go. Kissing her softly on the lips nothing could ruin his night. He was marrying the woman of his dreams.

Trent reluctantly let Shia go when his cell vibrating at his hip distracted him. Recognizing Kodi's mother's number, he quickly answered.

"Hello."

"William was found today."

Trent was ecstatic about the news. This meant that Phylicia must have finally come to her senses, but then why did Kodi's mother sound sad?

"That's good news right?" He asked cautiously.

"No," She began weeping on the other end of the line, "He was found on my doorstep with a gunshot wound to his little head. Whoever killed Sherri must have kept him for a few weeks then killed him."

Trent's body went numb when he heard the news. "She didn't." He whispered.

"What happened?" Shia asked in the background.

"Who didn't? You know who did this?" Kodi's mother voice was more amped now.

"I'm a have to call you back." Trent wasn't trying to be rude, but he disconnected the call. He had to contact Phylicia.

"What is going on?" Shia questioned.

Trent dialed Phylicia's number ignoring Shia's question for the time being.

"Yo P. what the fuck you do?" Trent shouted into the phone as soon as she answered.

"What are you talking about?" Phylicia asked calmly.

"You know exactly what I'm talking about. Why? Why did you do it?"

"Because, it was either that or turn myself in. Both his parents were dead anyway. There was no reason to keep him holding on asking for his mother and what not. I did him a favor and took him out of his misery, so he could join her and his dad in the afterlife. Now the whole family is together."

Trent looked down at his cell in disbelief because Phylicia was dead serious.

"You're not getting away with this shit."

"Too late, I already have and if you're thinking of going to the police, I would decide against that."

"I would hate for something unfortunate to happen to your new fiancée."

Trent abruptly snapped his neck up and begun looking around.

"Where are you?"

"Watching you. I saw the whole proposal. Trust me no wedding will ever take place. Even if you're not a betting man, you can bet on that." She said before she disconnected the call.

"What in the world Babe?"

Trent turned around to find Shia staring at him intensely. "Sounds like drama."

"No drama at all. Everything will be fine." That was the first lie he told his bride to be.

* * * *

"Marriage Shy? Are you sure you're ready for all that?"

"Yes, I'm ready." Shia looked at Leigh in anticipation, "Why what's your beef this time Leigh?"

"It's a little fast." Shia rolled her eyes.

"Here you go with this mess again. What do you mean fast? I've known Trent for years."

"Yeah, but y'all have a bad history of this on again off again thing."

"Well, thank you Dr. Phil, but I got this okay."

"Just saying, your last choice was garbage."

"As you repeatedly told me, but in that same argument, you were a Trent advocate. What has changed?"

"Nothing. I think Trent is the right choice. I'm just saying it seems really fast considering everything that has gone down recently with this family."

"It's because of everything that has gone down with us that I said yes. Life is too short and I love him. Don't want to waste another minute playing games."

Leigh suddenly smiled, "Music to my ears. You're making the right choice. Just wanted to make sure you knew you were."

"Aye, I'm the older twin. I got this." Shia said returning Leigh's smile displaying mirror
images of one another in harmony for the time being.

"I'm happy for you big sis." Leigh replied giving Shia a hug and kiss on the cheek. "So, when's the wedding?"

"Soon. I'm thinking next month."

"Whoo, stop the presses." Leigh exclaimed. Throwing her hands in the air. "Are you serious? How are we supposed to get a wedding popping in that amount of time?"

"It will all work out for the best. Oh ye of little faith trust me okay." Shia smirked with love in her eyes. We're going to rock it out."

Leigh laughed in the spirit of Shia's merriment. "Ok, ok. You've made me a believer. Let's get the party started."

* * * *

Phylicia knew she had gone a bit far by terminating William's life contract, but she didn't see how she had any other choice. If she'd returned him alive in one piece, he would have told his grandmother that he was with his God mommy the whole time and that she had visited their home before she took him. Phylicia just didn't need the drama, so he'd had to go. She felt as if she had done the right thing by returning his body to his grandmother's house so she could at least mourn and move on.

It was a month since Trent had phoned about William's death. She knew he'd gone to the funeral because she called Kodi's mother with her condolences. No one would or could ever understand her plight, but she had to do what she had to do.

She had more pressing matters to focus on today. Today was the day Trent thought he would be marrying Shia, but the two of them had another thing coming.

Dialing Trent's number, Phylicia waited patiently for him to answer.

Trent was excited. Today he was marrying the right woman for him and everything in his body was him this was the right decision for him. When Trent's phone rang his mood waivered however, when he saw Phylicia's name flash across his iPhone screen interrupting preparation for his wedding. He debated against answering, but against his better judgment wanted to see what she had to say.

"Yo, why you calling me?"

"I'm thinking about turning myself in."

Trent almost dropped the phone. This was monumental.

"Are you sure?" He asked.

"Yes, can I stop by first?"

"You really can't P. I have plans for the day."

"I know it's your wedding day. Don't worry; I'm not going to do anything to sabotage it. I just want to see you one last time before I go down to the station."

Trent thought long and hard. Phylicia knew he was hesitant. "Come on Trent. It won't take long. I just want to say good-bye."

"Ok." Trent found himself agreeing, "But it has to be quick."

"It will be, don't worry."

"Aight." He hung up.

While waiting for Phylicia to stop by, Trent dialed Shia's number and Leigh answered.

"Where the hell are you?" She yelled into the phone.

"Lemme speak to Shy." Trent ignored said ignoring Leigh's question.

"She's getting her make-up done and about to get dressed. I'll see you in a few." Then she hung up.

Trent sighed in frustration. He'd wanted to hear Shia's voice and tell her he loved her.

The concierge buzzed him. Phylicia arrived. Locking up his apartment because he didn't trust her Trent waited for her in the hallway. He shook his head as soon as Phylicia exited the elevator.

“How are you walking around the streets of New York like that?”

Phylicia was clad in see through lace from head to toe, showing off her banging body. Trent kept his gaze focused on her face.

“Like I care, but if you must know, I took my coat off on the elevator.”

“If you came to get some you came to the wrong place. I have to go.”

“You know you love me, don’t marry that girl.”

“She’s not a girl. She’s all woman and I’m out. I thought you stopped by to say good-bye, not this classless shit you pulling now.”

“Well at least if I can’t change your mind can I at the very least have a hug?”

Trent sighed hard. He was tired of playing games with Phylicia. He just wanted her to go away.

“Aight, one hug and then you need to go.”

“Yes Daddy, one hug.”

Trent shook his head in disgust as he gave Phylicia the hug she sought.

“Aight,” He said pulling out of her embrace, “We’re done here.”

“Yes, we are.” Phylicia said holding up his cell phone with amused eyes.

Trent glanced down at the empty phone clip on his hip.

“Aye, yo P quit playing. Give me my phone. You acting like a child.”

“Yeah, well since I’m acting like a child, come catch me.” She took off down the hall and entered the stairwell.

Trent let her go. He wasn’t interested in playing games. He could always get another phone, but he wasn’t interested in getting another fiancée. Headed toward the elevator, drama aside, he was ready to make Shia his wife.

Chapter Thirty-Two

Shia was sitting on the bathroom floor crying her eyes out. She wasn't in a position to take on any more drama. It was a trying year as it was for the entire family. The whole ordeal with Leigh and Remi being kidnapped. The fact that her ex-husband Demetri was one of her mother's lovers going by the name Maxwell and he actually was in love with her and since he couldn't have all of her he wanted to ruin her family and not to mention that he was Phylicia's ex-husband, the father of her daughter Avionne and her twins were Avionne's little brothers. The situation completely sickened Shia's stomach. It was all just a little too much.

"Go away." Shia yelled when a soft knock came on the door.

"Shy baby, it's me. Please talk to me." Was that Trent's voice she wondered?

The male voice penetrated through Shia's wallowing moment of self-pity.

"Why would I talk to you?"

"Because you love me and you know I would never stand you up on our wedding day."

"Oh yeah." Shia spat out unlocking and opening the bathroom door a crack, "Then why is Phylicia answering your phone? Talking about running you two's bath water. What is all that about?"

Trent shrugged, "She's psycho."

Shia shook her head in disbelief and disappointment. "Why would you even see her on your wedding day? You know how she feels about you. I think you're the psycho one for coming here thinking I would believe you."

Shia backed away from the door while Trent gently let himself into the bathroom closing the door behind him.

"Hey babe, give me a little more credit. I didn't stop by to see her. I had just called you to let you know how much I love you and couldn't wait to see you standing at the end of the aisle, but Leigh wouldn't give you the phone. She basically told me to get to the venue and hung up on me." His voice carrying a hint of amusement as he paused before continuing.

"Phylicia stopped by my house and went into this whole one-woman show professing her love for me and when I told her none of it mattered because I was finally marrying the woman made for me, she snatched my phone out of my hand and took off." Trent pulled Shia with her tear-streaked face into his arms.

"I would never hurt you like I did before. Don't you know that? There is nothing Phylicia can do for me anymore. Nothing."

Shia wanted to believe him. She really did, but he and Phylicia's history with one another was suspect. She didn't know what to believe.

Trent could see Shia's inner struggle. She was going to fight him the whole way. He knew it, but he had to find a way to make her believe him. There had to be a way.

"Call my phone." Trent said suddenly releasing Shia out of his embrace.

"No." She replied with a calm stone face.

"Shy, I love you. Do you understand that? Phylicia no longer means anything to me. "He picked Shia's cell up from the floor and handed it to her. "Call it please. For me, for us?" Trent implored.

Shia reluctantly dialed the number to Trent's cell.

"What do you want?" Phylicia's attitude laced voice huffed on the first ring, "What will it take for you to realize that there will be no wedding?"

Shia rolled her eyes at her audacity. She knew the day that she met Phylicia that the chick was low class no matter how pretty she presented herself.

"Where's Trent?"

"In the bathtub waiting for me, but that's our business, what can I do for you?"

"Want to hear something funny Phylicia?" Without waiting for a response, Shia continued, "Trent is standing right here with me as we speak. Say hey baby." Shia held the phone up to Trent's mouth.

"Hey P." He said into the cell.

Bringing the cell back to her mouth Shia laughed, "You are so delusional. You should she a psychiatrist about that."

The phone clicked on Phylicia's end without another word.

Sheepishly looking up at Trent Shia caught him smirking at her with an I told you so gleam in his eyes.

"Hmmn, would I seem to have an apology coming my way?" He asked looking down at her, "What will it take to have you fully trust me?"

"A lifetime." Shia answered honestly.

"Amazing," Trent whispered tipping her chin up so she was looking up at him, "I have one of those to give."

Shia blushed as she stared into Trent's eyes and realized that he meant it with his whole heart. Bending on one knee, Trent took Shia's hand in his.

"Shia Cunningham, will you marry me today with God as our witness in front of all our family and friends? I'd be honored if you'll allow me to be your husband and take care of you for the rest of your life."

Shia knew Trent was the real deal. Everything in her body was screaming he was the one. To gain a lot, one must risk a lot. Business Management 101.

"Yes." Shia said throwing her arms around his neck, "I can't wait to marry you." Shia pondered for a moment, "Only problem is I heard Remi say she was going to make an announcement to let everyone know the wedding was off."

Opening the bathroom door Trent gave Shia a tiny nudge toward the dressing room where Leigh and Remi were waiting.

"I got here just in time to put a stop to that announcement." Shia turned looking at Trent in amazement. He bent his head down and kissed her nose.

"As beautiful as you are in your sexy lingerie, I can't wait to see you in your white dress professing your undying love to the man of your dreams."

Shia couldn't contain it; try as she might; she burst out laughing.

"Seriously, man of my dreams? Please," She said waving him off, "Not hardly."

Trent grabbed her by the waist and lifted her off her feet so they were eye level.

"Tell me you love me."

"I love you!" A smiling Shia exclaimed, "Now get out of here so I can get dressed."

Trent returned her feet to the floor.

"Ok, meet you in thirty. I'll be the one in the front, praying for God to save me."

"I bet." A laughing Shia pushed him out of the door glancing at her sisters once he was gone.

"I'm glad Trent got himself together. I would have hated to F him up." Leigh said walking up to Shia with her reception dress in her hands.

"I know. We were about to handle that for you Shy." Remi chimed in.

Phylicia's still gonna get hers though. Believe that!" Leigh fumed.

"Ok you guys, no more talk about Phylicia. It's my wedding day and I've let her ruin it long enough. We're not going to make the whole day about her. We need to worry about the fact that now I have to wear my receptionist dress for the whole day now."

"Well, no one told your genius twin to cut you out of your gown." Remi said with a pointed look at Leigh.

"Hey!" Leigh exclaimed, "She said she couldn't breathe. I didn't want her to start hyperventilating."

"Come on you two enough." Shia turned to the mirror with a grin, "My future husband is waiting."

* * * *

Phylicia could see security monitoring the edge of the property where the wedding site was and she could hear the wedding taking place on the inside of the tent. Disguised in a jet-black bob wig with black rimmed personality glasses on, she was posing as a waitress for the reception. Slipping away from the wait staff unnoticed she made sure to keep her eye on the security guards. She had come to the site the day before to watch the security go throw they inspection of the grounds and to see where they would be holding up post during the event. Creeping around the 40x60 tent that was housing the wedding, Phylicia pulled gas cans that she had strategically placed in the shrubbery the day before. Glancing from side to side as she made sure to stay out of view of security, Phylicia began creeping around the tent dousing the tent with gas by the entry ways and on the sides. Removing a box of matches from the waitress apron that was tied around her waist, she lit one at time as she retraced her steps where she applied the gas. Momentarily mesmerized by the sight of the fire, Phylicia smiled in satisfaction and retreated into the trees to watch it all play out.

* * * *

Leigh had tears of happiness trailing from her eyes for her sister because Shia was beaming the entire time she said her vows to Trent and he seemed just as happy to be exchanging vows with her.

"You may now kiss your bride." The minister said.

Shia looked into Trent's eyes and melted. Those were the words that she was waiting all these years to hear. Her heart began doing flip-flops as she closed her eyes while he lowered his mouth to hers.

"OH MY GOD! The tent is on fire!" Remi's scream forced everyone into action.

"What!" Shia snapped her eyes open and turned her head towards Remi, before Trent had a chance to kiss her. She saw exactly what Remi meant when she glanced around the tent and saw that it was engulfed in flames.

"We have to go!" Trent yelled grabbing her hand in the midst of the chaos of people running around trying to find a way out the tent since all the entryways was blocked by fire.

"Go where?" We're trapped in here!" Shia yelled back cursing herself for having a wedding in a tent in the first place that was set on a structure stuck in place, as she began to choke on smoke.

"I have my blade." Remi screamed as she and Leigh ran behind Shia and Trent, "We're going to have to cut ourselves out."

Phylicia looked on from her hiding place at the burning tent admiring her handy work. Trent and Shia were crazy if they thought she was going to allow them to continue in wedding bliss and leave her hanging like this. Trent was the man she had to have and have him; she would, by any means necessary. She watched as some of the attendees found a way to free themselves from the tent as they were gasping for air. Hearing the sirens, in the distance, Phylicia was oblivious to everything else around her.

"Excuse me miss, are you okay?"

So focused on what was happening before her eyes Phylicia hadn't heard one of the security men creeping up behind her until he had spoken causing her to jump a little.

"Yes. I am fine. I made it out of harm's way just in time." She answered him maintaining her calm composure so he wouldn't suspect her of anything.

"That's good ma'am. I'm going to need you to follow me so we can have one of the EMT's check you out and get a statement from you if you choose to give one."

"Oh no Sir," Phylicia stated shaking her head, "I don't need to give a statement. I just want to go home and relax."

"I'm going to have to insist ma'am. It's my job to make sure everyone is kept safe and I want to ensure that you are in perfect condition before I let you leave the property."

Phylicia sighed, "Ok. I'll follow you down so the EMTs can check me out." She said giving in.

"Thank you for accommodating me ma'am."

"Jason, pick up. We got a situation down here in the tent. We need your help." A voice was saying through the radio that hung on a clip connected to his belt on his uniform.

As he bowed his head to retrieve the radio, Phylicia cautiously removed a knife that she had stashed in her apron during the wait staff orientation and stabbed him multiple times in his neck before he had a chance to radio his partner back.

Watching as his body crumbled to the ground, Phylicia quickly squatted and pulled him further into the trees. Removing the gun he had at his side as well as his shirt, she cut the sleeves off his shirt and bound his wrists and ankles together placing him in a fetal position. Setting the knife on the ground Phylicia quickly pulled her white, blood-stained shirt over her head and tucked it in her apron, turned his sleeveless shirt inside out and put it on then pulled out a match. Grabbing the sleeve that bound his hands, Phylicia lit one of the ends and walked away from the body knowing it was only a matter of time before they found his body.

* * * *

Movement to the far left of the tent along the perimeter of the trees grabbed Trent's attention. After making sure that Shia and her sisters were safely out of harm's way, Trent told Shia he would be back and walked towards the trees where he had seen the movement to investigate. As he walked closer to his destination, Trent could see a small cloud of smoke, it appeared to be thickening the closer he got to the source. Curiosity getting the best of him, he wanted to know the source of the smoke.

As Phylicia walked away from the security man's body it donned on her that she'd left the knife. Doing a swift about face turn, Phylicia quickly backtracked to the place where she had left the body.

Spotting a woman standing in the midst of the smoke source, Trent noticed a small fire and stopped short.

Hearing the footsteps behind her Phylicia quickly spun around ready to attack.

"Hey, there's smoke coming from the far side of the field." Trent heard someone yell in the distance.

"Phylicia?" Trent inquired. She looked like she was trying to disguise herself with the wig and glasses, but Trent would know her anywhere. "What the hell are you doing?" He asked looking down at the bloody body on the ground that was now almost completely covered in flames.

Retrieving her knife from off the ground Phylicia eyed Trent intently.

"You married that bitch anyway? After everything we've been through together, how could you do this to me?"

"P, you knew I was going to marry Shy."

"No," Phylicia said shaking her head, "You weren't supposed to go through with it. It was always supposed to be me and you." Phylicia said putting the knife in her apron and pulling out the gun.

"I love you, can't you see that? Khloe's death was supposed to bring us closer together. That was the plan?" She screamed with tears sliding down her face.

Trent looked at Phylicia as if she had two heads attached to her neck.

"Yo P, you bugging. You not making any sense." Trent was trying to make sense out of what she was telling him, "Are you saying that Khloe's death was planned?" He looked at her in hurt and anger. "You killed my daughter?" He yelled unable to keep the rage out of his voice.

Phylicia ignored his question. That's all you ever cared about was Khloe. What about me...us?"

Trent was angry and wanted to do Phylicia bodily harm, but she was pointing a gun at him. He had to figure out a way to get the gun out of her hands.

"Why didn't you just come and talk to me P?" He said softening his tone, trying to get her into a vulnerable state of mind, "We've always been able to talk to one another. You could have come to me and told me how you felt about me marrying Shia. I would have understood."

"Why did you propose to her anyway? I've been the consistent woman here in your life. I made one mistake, why couldn't you forgive me for it?"

"I forgave you a long time ago P. You never forgave you." He pointed out.

"If you forgave me, why couldn't we be together? I would have given you anything you wanted or needed."

Trent took a cautious step forward as she continued to point the gun at him, "I know you would have." He said taking another step forward, which brought him within touching distance of her. Raising his hand slowly he gently wiped the tears from her face. "We can still be together."

"How?" Phylicia whispered as she allowed him to wipe her tears, "You're already married."

"I can have the minister rip up the papers. They haven't been mailed to the state yet for processing." He pulled her into a hug, "Let me love you Phylicia." He said looking down into her wet eyes. Phylicia stared back up at him and when he lowered his head, she allowed him to kiss her.

While kissing her Trent reached up for the gun and she allowed him to take it. Trent deepened the kiss and Phylicia welcomed it moaning softly as she raised the knife she pulled out her apron and plunged it into Trent's back.

"Oh shit!" Trent screamed as he swayed on his feet.

"Did you think I would fall for that?" Phylicia screamed as she continued to stab him repeatedly in the back.

A shot rang out and Phylicia yelped in pain as she hit the ground hard.

"Help me, help me." She yelled grabbing her leg that the bullet was still lodged in.

Ignoring her words and obvious pain, the police officers roughly turned her over and handcuffed her then left her there as the EMTs felt Trent's wrist to make sure his unmoving body was still alive.

"I feel a faint pulse. Let's get him out of her." One of the EMTs said as his team came over and lifted him on the gurney then rolled him back to the ambulance.

While Trent was being rolled to the ambulance, the officers also allowed the EMTs to put Phylicia on a gurney; still handcuffed and rolled to another waiting ambulance to treat the bullet wound in her leg.

"What is taking Trent so long?" Shia said to her sisters, "He said he was going to check on something and would be right back."

"I don't know. I overheard one of the EMTs saying something was going on over on the far side of the grounds. See?" Leigh said pointing to the EMTs rushing in their direction with two gurney's in tow.

The closer the EMT's came, Shia could recognize the Armani pants that the person on the gurney was wearing.

"Oh my god! That's Trent." Shia exclaimed jumping up from the chair she was sitting in and running over to the ambulance, they were putting him in.

"That's my husband. I'm riding with him." Shia said in a chocked up voice and a face full of tears, "Is he going to be okay?" She took a glance at Trent unmoving body in the ambulance.

"Ma'am, you can't ride back here. You can join the driver in the front." Observing Shia's face crumbling even more the EMT softened his tone, "We're going to do everything we can to make sure he's alright."

"Jimmy." He said turning to another EMT tech, "Can you escort this lady up to the seat in front so she can ride with her husband to the hospital?'

"Sure thing. Ma'am, follow me." Shia followed the man to the front of the ambulance and got in next to the driver as he closed the door behind her and they sped off. Shia took the time to send up a silent prayer that her husband made it out of this alive.

Epilogue

The past year was a trying one. Some days, Shia wanted to voice complaints, but no one would care anyway so there was no point. After what she and Trent had endured on their wedding day, she really shouldn't have any complaints. Her man had survived his attacker and though he walked with a slight limp due to a little nerve damage in his back that in itself was a blessing. Even now, she found it hard to swallow that a mother would take the life of her own child in an effort to bring herself closer to the father of their child as they mourned a loss together. She didn't know who besides Phylicia thought like that. No child should have a mother that selfish. If only they could save Khloe from her deranged mother. Phylicia was sentenced to a mental ward. Shia hoped that was good enough. Phylicia needed someone who could help her deal with all her mental issues once and for all. To this day Phylicia still hadn't explained how she had taken Khloe's life, but Shia took small solace in believing they would know soon. An autopsy was in the works; Shia and Trent were patiently waiting to see what the outcome would be. Every time Shia thought about Phylicia taking the life of her own flesh and blood. It brought tears to her eyes. Placing a protective had over her swollen belly. She was due with her and Trent's first baby in a few months and couldn't be happier. She was finally getting a girl and the boys were ecstatic about being big brothers. And like any true mother, Shia couldn't wait to see them all playing together.

Going into her home office, sitting at her desk Shia took out a pen and paper, as she sometimes did in her alone time and began to draft a letter. Ten minutes later Shia stood from the desk to arch her back and retrieve an envelope and stamp. Placing her finished letter in the envelope, she sealed it and walked it down to the mailbox so it could go out today. Squealing in merriment when she felt the baby kick, she excitedly added as much pep to her step as she could at seven months to get back into the house as fast as she could so Trent could feel her belly.

* * * *

Phylicia glanced up as an envelope was shoved under her door. Walking over the cold floor barefoot, she bent down to pick it up off the floor. Looking at the envelope carefully she saw that there was no return address listed.

Sitting on her bed, Phylicia was loathe to open her only communication with the outside world and have it end in a matter of seconds. Placing the envelope on the bed, she lay next to it wondering who would have sent her something. She was holed up in an inpatient mental health hospital for the past nine months and felt like they were the reason she was going crazy. All the white in this place was enough to make anyone crazy, even if the thought they were sane upon admittance. Unable to take the suspense of what was in the envelope any longer, Phylicia sat up and tore open the letter.

Phylicia,

Amazing how the tables have turned. Who would have thought that things would turn out the way that they did? I'm a God fearing woman, so it is only right that I say to you that I will pray for you because it is the appropriate thing to do. But between you and me, you got what you deserved and every day you have to live with the undying fact that he loves me, he loves you not.

Forever and Always Trent's,
Shia, (Trent's one and only love.")

Feeling something else in the envelope, she turned it over and a photo dropped out. Picking up the photo Phylicia looked.

"Dumb motherfuckin' BITCH!" Phylicia screamed as she threw the photo down and began banging her head on the wall. "I'M GOING TO KILL THAT BITCH!" She yelled at the top of her lungs as she continued banging her head on the wall.

Hearing the commotion out in the hall, members of the hospital staff came to her room and unlocked the door to find Phylicia with a bleeding gash on her head and continuing to bang her head repeatedly on the wall despite the gash. The team ran in and restrained her before she could do more damage to herself. One gave her a tranquilizer to get her to calm down. Strapping her down to the bed, they left Phylicia in the room. The last staff member saw the photo on the floor, picked it up and placed it next to Phylicia's night stand so it could be the first thing she saw when she finally settled back into her normal state.

Waking a few hours later to a throbbing headache Phylicia couldn't understand why she was still strapped down. Glancing around her room the photograph she threw earlier stared back at her. Phylicia's eyes widened as she began screaming hysterically as her body jerked under the straps that held her thrashing body in place. She continued to scream hysterically into the night as the sonogram photo of Shia and Trent's baby continued to stare back at her.

About The Author

A native of the Metropolitan of Washington, DC, Mychea has had a dream to have her words shown in print since the age of eleven, when she began a series of illustrations and short stories. In April 2007, Mychea decided it was time to stop fantasizing and begin achieving, opting to turn her dreams into a reality and so her debut novel Coveted began.

She is the author of urban fiction novels He Loves Me, He Loves You Not, Coveted and Vengeance and Playwright of her stage play Coveted. In her spare time, Mychea loves to draw, model, act and plan events. She is hard at work on her next novel and stage play. You can view more about the author at www.mychea.com

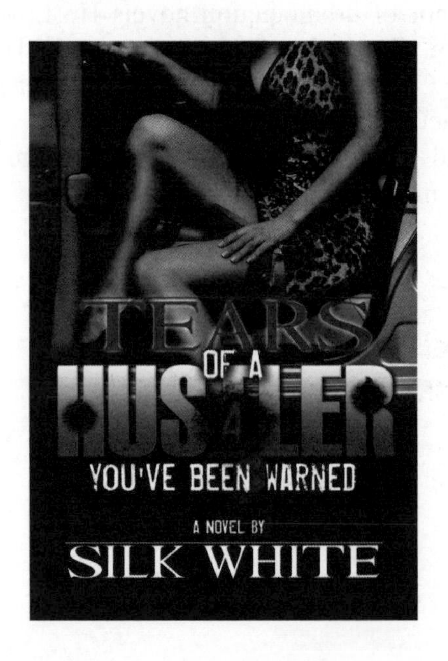

ALSO AVAILABLE THANKSGIVING NOV 22 2012

GOOD 2 GO PUBLISHING PRESENTS
PETALS OF DECEIT...
HE LOVES ME
HE
LOVES YOU NOT
A NOVEL BY MYCHEA

GOOD 2 GO PUBLISHING PRESENTS
NEVER
BE THE SAME
A NOVEL BY
SILK WHITE

THE
TEFLON
QUEEN
A NOVEL BY
SILK WHITE

GOOD 2 GO PUBLISHING PRESENTS
A NOVEL BY
SILK WHITE
MARRIED
to da
STREETS
AN URBAN CLASSIC TALE

Good2Go Publishing
Presents
TEARS
OF A
HUSTLER
A NOVEL BY
SILK WHITE

TEARS
OF A
HUSTLER
2
A NOVEL BY
SILK WHITE

GOOD 2 GO PUBLISHING PRESENTS
TEARS
OF A
HUSTLER
3
A NOVEL BY
SILK WHITE

Good2go Publishing Order Form

Last Name ______________________________

First Name ______________________________ M.I. ______

Address ______________________________ Apt./Unit ______

City ________________ State ____ ZIP Code ____________

Phone ( ) ______________ E-Mail ______________________

Method of payment ❑ Check ❑ VISA ❑ MasterCard

Credit Card # ______________________________ Exp. Date ______

Name as it appears on card ______________________________

____

Signature

Item Name	Price	Qty.	Amount
TEARS OF A HUSTLER (AUTHOR SILK WHITE)	13.95		
TEARS OF A HUSTLER PT 2	13.95		

(AUTHOR SILK WHITE)			
TEARS OF A HUSTLER PT 3 (AUTHOR SILK WHITE)	13.95		
TEARS OF A HUSTLER PT 4 (AUTHOR SILK WHITE)	13.95		
NEVER BE THE SAME (AUTHOR SILK WHITE)	13.95		
THE TEFLON QUEEN (AUTHOR SILK WHITE)	13.95		
MARRIED TO DA STREETS (AUTHOR SILK WHITE)	13.95		
HE LOVES ME, HE LOVES YOU NOT (AUTHOR MYCHEA)	13.95		
Subtotal			
Tax			
Shipping (FREE) U.S. MEDIA MAIl			
Total			

MAKE CHECK PAYABLE:

GOOD2GO PUBLISHING
7311 W GLASS LANE
LAVEEN, AZ 85339